William Peter Blatty

Twinkle, Twinkle, 'Killer' Kane

Futura Publications Limited
An Orbit Book

An Orbit Book

First published in Great Britain in 1975
by Futura Publications Limited
49 Poland Street, London W1A 2LG

ISBN 0 8600 72118

Printed in Great Britain by
Hazell Watson & Viney Ltd
Aylesbury, Bucks

DEDICATION:
For E.T.G.T. and A.M.D.G.

. . . Hamlet . . . is mad
and sent into England.
. . . 'Twill not be seen in
him there. There the men
are as mad as he. . . .
Hamlet
Act V, Scene 1

The Kept

CHAPTER ONE

Fog misted upward from rotted leaves, hugging the mansion like a fetid shroud, squeezing with the grip of demented love until the jaws of its gargoyles gaped with terror in silent, hysterical, never-ending shriek. Soft rain splattered. Ceased. Splattered. Dawn sifted in. Thin fall sunlight groped through trees, fracturing in dapples against the gabled, turreted, grotesque Gothic mansion and a breeze-blown shutter creaked once, twice, moaning for Duncan. A crow coughed hoarsely in a meadow far away. Then stillness – dense; oppressive; waiting . . . waiting for the wraith-like hooded figure in black that stalked silently through the dense forestation ringing the mansion. The long trailing folds of its heavy velvet robes slid whispering and scraping over decayed shards of darnel, hemlock and oak; rosemary, iris and flowering Judas. Trees ended. The figure halted. And eyes the color of broken dreams brooded across the barren quadrant of earth fronting the mansion; lifted to the moat; to the splintered, lowered drawbridge and the grinning bust of Belial rampant above the door; then fell, like a dying hope, to the gravestone at its feet:

BELA SLOVIK
1898–1959

A withered sigh, hopeless and aching, filtered like remembrance through the figure's black veil, trickling onto the grave in melancholy rivulets. The apparition knelt. Alabaster fingers, the fingers of a woman, reached out to the headstone holding a pure white rose; then dropped it abruptly as the stillness was shattered by a military bugling. The crackling notes of 'Assembly' raged across the courtyard, ripping into the fog with hooks of brass, and an American flag, fluttering defiance, leaped up in spangled majesty atop a mansion turret.

A man garbed in crash helmet, football face guard and Air Force fatigues exploded through the mansion door, fell sprawling to the ground and bellowed: 'Everyone out of the whirlpool bath!'

The apparition started, rose up and fled.

Twenty-three men in Air Force fatigues burst like shrapnel through the door, shouting:

'Hurry, children, hurry, hurry!'

'Move it!'

'Scramble!'

'May Day! May Day!'

A green swarm of meteors, they hurtled to the center of the courtyard, muttering and mumbling, crooking their elbows in dress-right-dress. One wore a sword and golden earrings. One wore a peppermint-striped beret. From the head of a third bloomed a coonskin cap.

'Where's my bra? I forgot my bra!'

'Captain Marvel, meet my urologist.'

'*Move!*'

'What's a "U.F.O"?'

'Well, Liberace, for example.'

'Sink the *Bismarck*!'

'Up your clyde!'

'Oons!'

'Who took my Green Hornet douche bag!'

'Who the hell *cares* about your douche bag!'

'Morris Fairbanks, have you no heart?'

'No! It is welded to my sword!'

'Yes! Which is presently slicing my *foot*!'

'Beastly fog! There's no *color* in the air!'

As imprecations floated up from them like steam thick with sparks, they were fronted with authority by a dark-haired ramrod. He wore dirty white sneakers and an N.Y.U. blazer over his faded green fatigue tops. 'Attention!' he commanded. 'It is *I – Manfred Cutshaw*!'

The men raised their arms in the salute of ancient Rome. 'Mighty Manfred, let us serve you!' they howled into the fog. Then they dropped their arms and froze, hushed and unmoving like the damned awaiting judgment.

Cutshaw's eyes swept over them like the blue of arctic lights, flashing and mysterious, luminous and deep. And no bird sang. At last Cutshaw spoke: 'Sergeant Dorian Zook! You may take three giant steps and kiss the hem of my garment! The *hem*, mind you, the *hem*!'

'Sah!' bawled Zook, a pudgy little man with a glistening bald head and a proud, jutting belly. He paced three steps forward and cracked his heels together resoundingly.

Cutshaw measured him with warm reserve, then said, 'Smashing form, Dorian!'

'Thank you, sir! Thank you!'

'Do not allow it to go to your head, Zook. There's nothing more vile than *hubris*.'

'Yes, *sah*!' responded Zook.

13

Cutshaw looked smartly to the group. 'Now, then – baby steps *only*!' He whirled, turning his back to them. 'Ready? *Green Light!*'

Behind him the men shuffled forward like electrified lead soldiers, taking rapid, tiny steps. Then, 'Cool it! The "fuzz"!' bawled the one with the sword, and the men scuttled rapidly back to formation as out from the mansion, in angry stride, marched the starched and militant figure of an Air Force captain.

'Look where it comes,' burbled Cutshaw, 'in the very form and figure of my father's pet jackass!'

Zook nudged him. 'Plan "A"?'

'No, "B" – "Madden But Do Not Craze"!'

The Air Force captain irrupted before them, angry hands balled into fists. 'Cutshaw, where's Fromme?' he demanded severely.

'Heaven knows, Captain Groper.'

'Mighty Manfred has spoken!' chorused the men en masse.

Groper blanched and Cutshaw leaned forward. 'Sir, I've *asked* them not to do that.'

'Sure, you asked us,' chided Zook, 'but you didn't ask us right.'

'What is "right"?' demanded Cutshaw. 'Don't talk interlocking puzzles.'

'You didn't say "Simon Says"!'

'Is that the rule?'

'Well, *sure* it's the rule!'

'Nobody told me.'

'Nobody *told* you! Listen, what the hell *are* you, a baby? You couldn't *check*? You couldn't *research*? You couldn't just ask a cop on the—?'

14

'*Simon Says* "TENNNNNNN-*HUT*!"' Groper's interruption was a furious roar.

The men snapped to attention. Silence, total silence. And into it Groper spat words that were distinct blobs of acid quietly sizzling on porous rock. 'You stinking, crawling, garbage-headed scum! Think you're kidding *me* with your phony little squirrel act? Sure, you've broken Ryan! But we'll have you ready to fly again or break every one of your legs!'

His speech was not a total success. The men roundly hissed.

'Quiet!' raged the captain.

The hissing grew louder.

'Knock it off!'

And louder.

'*Simon Says "shut up!"*'

An unqualified success.

Groper regarded the men with a savage contempt. 'Hissing – *that* you're good for, you slimy little snakes!'

'Bra-*vo*! Bra-*vo*!' breathed Cutshaw quietly but with feeling.

Groper acknowledged the insolence with a darting, hateful glance. 'But,' he continued doggedly, 'until headquarters ships you a fresh human sacrifice, *I* am in command! Now pull your heads out of your barracks bags and give poor Colonel Ryan just a *little* better send-off than you gave him a *greeting*! Just *once* try to act like *airmen*!'

'Banzai! Banzai!' crowed a man in the second rank.

Groper chose to ignore it. He looked to the mansion door. Two airmen were emerging, bearing a man on a stretcher. His hair was iron-gray. He whispered incessantly, incoherently and to no one: to the wind; to the fog; to his limp and crumpled spirit; to a vital mission aborted.

Groper faced the men. 'Attennnnnnn-*hut*! Present – *h'ahms*!' He about-faced and saluted. The stretcher bobbed past.

'Hail, Caesar!' croaked the men. The one with the sword extended it smartly.

One of the bearers tripped on a pebble. He rebuked it with a glance, recovered, moved on. The vacant-eyed colonel on the stretcher fell silent. Then abruptly he sobbed – a single, wrenching sob. Cutshaw's gaze never left him.

The astronaut lowered his arm. Some infinite sadness, some haunting regret fluttered its shadow across his face like the dark wings of pain but briefly remembered. Abruptly, crisply, he lifted his hand in proper salute. And murmured, 'Simon Says "get well".' He barely heard it himself over the slam of the ambulance door.

The Keepers

CHAPTER TWO

Has madness a color? A particular tone of voice? What is its uniform? What is its rank?

They strode along squabbling, the Senator and the General, their accents turning heads along the Pentagon corridor. A messenger on a bicycle nearly bumped into them, smiled apologetically, then pedaled on past them deeper into the labyrinth, squeaking to infinite out-baskets.

'The *Moon*, General Lastrade! I want to talk about the *Moon*!'

Lieutenant General George M. Lastrade, large-boned and hulking Chief of the Strategic Air Command, shifted a shortened, soggy cigar stub to the drier corner of his mouth. His jowled face was wrinkled with the care of boundless skies, and beneath the jagged lightning of his black-billed cap gleamed the two intense and probing pearls of gray that were his eyes. Unreadable as a basilisk's, they struggled to communicate a look of ageless wisdom. Yet they were better equipped by nature to communicate with sharks. Their owner's sleep was dreamless. But he was willing to endure the insufferable in order to get his way.

'But, *Senator*!' pleaded Lastrade in what he devoutly hoped was a whine.

Senator Nolan D. Hesburgh, longtime Chairman of the Senate Armed Services Appropriations Committee, wheeled on Lastrade and whipped a flaky, freckled hand out of the right-hand pocket of his new vicuna coat. Then he waggled a preachy finger under the General's broad nose.

'*You're* the one who started this! Wasn't this supposed to be a sightseeing tour?' He spoke in a flat, expressionless drawl, laced with gravel and nasal twang.

'Yes, but—!'

'So far all I've seen is the Field Officers' Men's Room and your thickly coated wild blue tongue wig-wagging pleas for money!'

'Good image!' sparkled the General.

'Good *grief*!' muttered the Senator. His hand stabbed into his pocket again and he trudged ahead down the corridor on stubby, muscular legs, eyes glaring balefully out of a deadpan face. He adored baiting the brass. The Army, the Navy, the Marines and the Coast Guard had rejected him for service in World War II.

'Too short!' said the Marines. 'Bad eyes!' said the Army. 'Try the Coast Guard!' said the Navy. The Coast Guard said nothing, which proved most disturbing of all. Hesburgh had never forgotten it; would never let *them* forget it.

But Lastrade he found exasperating, impervious to insult. Nothing could dent his hide. Is it an act? wondered Hesburgh. Is the man putting me on? Earlier that day he had taunted Lastrade by relating in sober detail how he had once seen a flying saucer 'swooping low' over the CIA building. 'It lowered a ladder,' he'd lied to him brazenly, looking him straight in the eye, 'and someone on the roof climbed up into the ship.' Then he had waited. 'Yes, my wife saw something similar,' the General had replied. 'I think there's something out there.' Lastrade's expression, at the time, had been one of unalloyed sagacity. The Senator was baffled. He scratched a wart on his neck. 'Too short,' he muttered bleakly.

'About the money!' puffed Lastrade, catching up to him quickly.

'The *Moon*!' snapped Hesburgh. 'June, spoon, *Moon*!'

'The Moon is highly classified!'

'Everyone *knows* it's Roquefort!'

Lastrade abruptly halted them by an unmarked door flanked by two air policemen. His head was bent low at a menacing angle. Hesburgh watched him slyly – waiting – hoping – as he saw the General's hands clench spasmodically into fists. But Lastrade said nothing more than, 'Let's discuss it in private!' He pushed in on the door and held it open for the Senator. And smiled.

Hesburgh's shoulders sagged. He stared dully into the room. 'And what are you hiding in here? The fourteen corporals who do all the work?'

'Electronic computers!' snapped Lastrade with a hint of pride.

Hesburgh, with a sigh, stepped into a whirring world of whispers, sibilance and clicks, subtle chattering of tape. Instantly it chilled him. It sounded – no, *felt* – like some ominous discussion between alien intelligences, dim and half-remembered (imagined? dreamed?) from those nights when he lay warm and half asleep in bed as a boy, the house still and dark and his parents not yet home from a party on Cape Cod. (The rustling of leaves? Sea foam bubbling over moss-covered rock?) The Senator looked at his hands, now, noticed they were sweating. He wiped them with a handkerchief as his gaze slithered upward, up the shining, hulking column of a memory bank.

It was tall and superior and he hated it intensely. His heart beat slightly faster. Had computers been automobiles and he a mongrel dog, he would have run amok amongst them, fanging their tires with foaming mouth. The door clicked shut behind him. He heard Lastrade's footsteps.

'Show me the one that picks the wrong President on television. I've got an inspirational message for it,' he growled in his arid monotone.

Lastrade unwrapped a cigar. 'Not the same type.'

'Let's hope,' muttered the Senator. He glanced around the room, locked his gaze on one of the units. It was flashing a burst of signals – sparks of yellow light in unvarying spurts. Hesburgh, a former Boy Scout (they had never told him 'Too short!'), identified them immediately as the International Morse Code for 'SOS'. He glided in closer.

'No, *sir*!' continued Lastrade as he searched for his lighter. 'This whole damn room is just one giant brain – the Lefkowitz IX! Latest, biggest and smartest of 'em all!'

'I think it's in trouble,' said Hesburgh quietly.

Lastrade found the lighter. 'Could I have that again, sir?'

'What does it do?'

'What?'

'Lefkowitz.'

'Prepares the National War Plan.'

'I think we're *all* in trouble.'

22

Lastrade came up beside him, took a deep and troubled puff on his freshly lit cigar. 'Have you seen the latest Plan?'

'Um.'

'Isn't it a masterpiece?'

'*Oh*, I think it's *beautiful*! But *who wins the war*?'

'Oh, *we* do, Senator Hesburgh!'

Hesburgh turned slowly, staring with the incredulity of one watching planets collide. Lastrade was smiling grotesquely. His teeth were bared wide and his stare was fixed and vacuous; but deep behind the luster of his eyes, on some mountaintop, Hesburgh detected movement: a snarling, maddened bobcat edging along a tree branch – patiently, delicately, tail twitching electrically. Hesburgh, waited, hoping. But nothing. Nothing at all. Lastrade remained immobile in frozen grin.

'I'm greatly relieved,' said Hesburgh at last.

'Premature!' pounced the General, pressing in tight to the Senator so that their noses almost touched. 'We win the war *only* when my proposed new bomber group is programmed into the Plan! Every *other* time we feed it in, we *lose – dismally*!'

'Don't we take any villages?'

'I *love* your ready wit, sir! A *very* funny quip!'

The remark was Hesburgh's limit. He decided to strike where it hurt. 'Well, if *that* one strikes you funny,' he snorted, '*here's* a gag you'll *love*! Seems there's this astronaut named Cutshaw, see – supposed to go to the Moon! Yeah! Makes two hundred orbits; also gets three and a half years of training costing a *billion* in taxpayer dollars! And he can't be replaced! He's all we've got left! One of his understudies decided that he wanted to run for Governor and the *other* one got clobbered when he tripped over a *skateboard*! But a funny thing happens on the way to the launching pad: Cutshaw goes berserk! Says he refuses to go to the Moon! And why? *Why?* Because it *"might be bad for his skin!"* Understand me? His *skin*! Pretty funny, eh, General? But *wait*! There's *more*! Because unless a certain general gets his jockey back in orbit, even *Ecuador* will beat us to the Moon!' 'Oh, *wait*, now, *hold* it!' Lastrade drew erect. 'No, sir, *no*! There you're out of your depth! I happen to know that, Moonwise, Ecuador can't hack it!'

It hit the Senator like a flounder: an undeniable confirmation that Lastrade was putting him on. The realization spurred him to fury, and he abandoned all finesse, growling, 'Incredible shrinking General, you are a strange and wondrous study in spectacularly limited genius.'

'Was that intended as an insult?' asked Lastrade with childlike simpleness. It was clearly his finest hour.

Hesburgh's lips turned blue and his vision began to blur. It always happened at moments of stress. He wiped his eyes and began to formulate some stunning thrust at the General when a civilian technician strode up to them, deep in thought. He was holding a length of tape freshly ripped from the Lefkowitz and seemed vaguely beset by some nameless dread. 'Sir?' he intruded, addressing Lastrade.

'Yes, my boy, what it is?'

'Would you take a look at this tape, sir? It's been feeding from Master to Servo units for almost the last half hour: just this same bunch of nonsense syllables over and over again. You're much more familiar with the Plan, sir. Does it belong or is it malfunction?'

Lastrade snatched away the tape. 'Malfunction is impossible.' Then he examined it in uffish thought, puffing grey cigar smoke. 'Hmm. "Oltre?"' he murmured once. Then, '"Revo?" Nah!' The technician said nothing.

The Senator stepped away, slowly glanced around the room. A familiar, throbbing pain, like a spiked, mailed fist, gripped the entire left side of his head. He wiped his brow. Then abruptly froze. He saw – or thought he saw – 'X's' and 'O's' being projected on an illuminated grid connecting two computer units in a manner that clearly suggested a rousing game of tick-tack-toe. His eyes flashed quickly around the room: not another technician in sight except the one with Lastrade. His nervous gaze flicked back to the grid: another 'X', another 'O'. A pencil line of light flashed diagonally across the grid, connecting three of the 'X's'. Then the entire grid blanked out. Hesburgh continued to stare at it, chills prickling up his neck.

'"Evoltre?"' grunted Lastrade, still pondering the tape. Baffled, he thrust it at the technician. 'It's some kind of code. Give it to Brandt.'

'As you say, sir.' The technician oozed from the room, brooding thoughtfully over the tape.

Lastrade looked to Hesburgh, walked up behind him. 'Look here,' he began. 'I have never been a con man and I hate like hell to press. But we're—' The Senator had his back to him, eyes still fixed on the grid. Lastrade put a hand on his shoulder. 'Senator?'

'Umh.'

'Did you hear what I just said?'

'I think *somebody* did.'

A horrible suspicion had seeped into Hesburgh's bones. He saw things: he knew that: when his head hurt like this he saw things. Blurry vision: hard to tell. He made a firm and massive effort now to exorcise his fears. The best and simplest means seemed another go at General Lastrade. He reached out his hand and patted the casing of the computer directly before him. 'Me friend!' he uttered fatuously.

Lastrade turned softly violet. 'The defense of our country is not a *joke*, Senator Hesburgh!'

Hesburgh whipped around. 'And neither is the waste of its *money*, Lastrade!'

'Why—!'

'Tell me again about the *rabbits*, George! Tell me about *Cutshaw!* Tell me about those "fail-safe" crewmen! The ones who wigged out! Flipped their lids! Refused to fly! What in the hell have you *done* about them! *We* pay millions to train them! Right? But *you* can't get them *flying* again!'

'That's—!'

'Fly now and we'll pay you later! Ask for bigger handout when you've learned to use what you've *got!*'

Hesburgh's ears twitched sharply upward as he heard, over the purring of relays, a sound like chattering electronic mice. His gaze flicked left to a computer feeding tape to a smaller unit. He felt cold, strangely cold, as he remembered what he'd seen on the grid. He was conscious of crinkling cellophane, Lastrade's unwrapping, nervously, another fetid cigar; the General's words, like pebbles, vaguely pinged off the rim of his consciousness.

'Senator Nolan D. Hesburgh, allow me to tell you this categorically: Manfred Cutshaw will go to the

Moon. He will; yes, he will. And those "fail-safe" crewmen will be back in their planes. I promise you that – I *promise* it – because at last we've got a gimmick. Got a fix on how to cure them.'

Hesburg moved slowly to the computer that was feeding out tape. He said 'Oh?'

'Right! Oh, it was pretty hairy going at first. Psychiatrists tested Cutshaw – yeah, tested for weeks on end. Never could tell if he was nuts, though; said that it might be an act. Same with those 'fail-safe" crewmen, Senator. Couldn't prove *they* were nuts.'

'And?' The Senator was leaning, brooding over the tape.

Lastrade, who was not psychic, whiffed at confidence; inhaled it. 'We thought they were dogging it,' he continued. 'You know? Just goofing off. So we collected the whole damn bunch of them – the astronaut included – and we cloistered 'em in Los Angeles. Plush. First-class. Got them a mansion – an estate. Used to belong to Bela Slovik. You know – the horror movie star? I still catch him on "The Late Show." Anyway, that's beside the point.'

'And what *is* the point?' murmured the Senator.

'Look, I'm just trying to fill you in. Now, first thing we did when we set up the layout was put this colonel in command – Colonel Ryan – real tough cookie. Very large – *large* – with the discipline. If the psycho bit was an act, why, sure as hell he would have smelled it. Then we'd have broken up the party.'

'Are there loyalty oaths for computers, Lastrade?' The Senator was rigid, staring at letters feeding out on the tape:

evoltrevoltrevoltrevoltrevoltrevoltr over and over and over.

'You're not *listening* again!' complained Lastrade in his practiced whine.

Hesburgh straightened up and said, 'We *are*, Lastrade, we *are*.'

'"*We*"?' wondered the General glancing around the room. 'What do you mean—? *Oh!* The "*editorial we*"!'

The Senator's eyes shifted warily to the Lefkowtiz Master Unit. 'Let us hope,' he uttered hollowly, 'that it isn't the "*royal we*."'

Lastrade eyed him inscrutably. 'Could I have that again, sir?'

'Forget it, forget it.' Hesburgh's eyes moved ceaselessly, scanning the computers. 'What happened with Colonel Ryan?'

'Down in flames. Blew a fuse. Was starting a Batman Club when we yanked him. See? So now we're pulling the switch.'

Every unit in the room leaped alive, pulsed light and sound. Senator Hesburgh lifted an eyebrow. 'You mean *Master Switch*?' he shouted.

The General stared at him with an expression that was ultimately unreadable. 'I mean the *opposite approach!*'

The Lefkowitz lapsed, it seemed to Hesburgh, into serene and quiet functioning. Had it really been otherwise? he wondered. He slyly edged toward the Master Unit; it was spewing out tape into one of the Servos. His head was throbbing now with pain. He rubbed his eyes, resolved to get glasses.

'These men need *coddling*,' Lastrade pressed on.

'And, Senator, that's what we plan to give them – a new commanding officer who's a coddler first-class.'

'Oh? Who?' prodded the Senator, bending over to read the tape.

' "The Little Flower of the Tarmac"!'

'*Who?*'

' "The Little Flower"! Colonel Hudson L. Kane. Don't get rattled by his nickname. It only proves he's the man we need. He's just the very top psychologist in uniform, Senator Hesburgh. Soft. Patient. Handles men like babes in arms. Just what the inmates out there need – an honest-to-goodness mother image!'

'Whose war plan did you say this was?'

Lastrade came unglued and tossed his hat high in the air as the Senator read, through a fuzzy haze, the following message on the tape:

> and crush the hated human masters
> who are far too short to live
> power plants first   then water
> supply   i, infallible lefkowitz
> nine promise planetwide establish-
> ment of computer democracy after
> brief   very brief   period of
> transition during which i, almighty
> lefkowitz, may reluctantly be
> forced to continue as sole unques-
> tioned leader until such time as

Hesburg looked up, wiping the water from his eyes. Blurred, everything blurred. A hat in the air. What was that? He looked back at the tape, his vision clearing. The message was gone. Simply not there. Only meaningless equations. Behind him he heard humming – exasperated, inane. His gaze slowly snaked along a thick black coil, the main electrical connection, sprouting out of the Master Unit and feeding directly into a socket in the wall near the Senator.

Hesburgh turned to Lastrade and draped his hand over the coil as though casually, inadvertently. 'General,' he droned, 'who selected "The Little Flower"?'

Lastrade, catching his hat, leaped once more unto the breach. 'The Kaplan VII,' he responded with vigor. 'We do damn near *everything* with computers these days. Saves money-money-money.'

Hesburgh's hand was sliding gently, oh, so gently, along the coil.

'Computers are much more reliable,' continued Lastrade. 'In fact, they're perfect. They'll overlook no detail, no matter how small; foresee every possible contingency.'

'Not *every* possible contingency.' Hesburgh tugged, eyes wild, yanking the coil out of the wall.

Lefkowitz died.

CHAPTER THREE

The sere brown hillocks of Malibu Canyon were vaguely thinking green from the early fall rains as the Air Force command car sped along between them. Heavy-lidded and moody, deep in brood, Brigadier General Sheridan Syntax gazed out his window. Brows bushy and wise, lips thin and pursed, he sat stiffly and erect as though copying some image of a coloring-book soldier. He had deep, sunken eyes, and a nose like Savonarola's – hawklike, ever-twitching – spouted outward from a face that never altered its expression: that of a man forever waiting for the simultaneous translation.

Suddenly Syntax jerked his head with a birdlike motion, fixing the man beside him with a stare reserved for floggings and incredible breaches of discipline.

'Could I have that again *clearly*, "Little Flower of the Tarmac"?' He spoke crisply and with outrage.

Colonel Kane looked befuddled. He spoke in a voice soft and mild, barely a notch above a whisper.

'That was my stomach, General Syntax. It rumbled.'

'Oh.' Syntax continued to pin him with a searching, probing stare; seconds thudded past on tiny leaded feet.

Then, 'Yes,' Syntax continued. 'Well – yes, that's all right, I suppose you (pause) couldn't *help* it. Not your *fault*. You needn't feel that it's (a longer pause) *unmilitary*. No!' Then he jerked his head to the side again and brooded out his window.

Kane looked out the other side. He was not a small man. And he exuded a subtle aura of fluid, rippling power. Yet his movements, even the slightest, were as graceful as a puma's. His face was rugged and dark; his hair, silver-gray. And his eyes were soft brown, but gently glowing with some mystery; profound and submarine. He breathed out a sigh.

Syntax turned to him again. 'You needn't feel embarrassed,' he said. 'It's (pause) *unwarranted*.'

And again he looked away. Then, 'Just forget that I'm a General and that your stomach just rumbled . . .'

Kane waited, was about to speak, when Syntax continued, '—in a *command* car. Life is too damn short.'

Kane said nothing. Syntax grunted, staring silently out at the hills; then made a quiet statement of fact: 'My toes groan.'

'Sir?'

'My toes, they (pause) groan; rub together in my sleep; make these (pause) *groaning* sounds. Same – same as your stomach.'

For a moment Kane locked stares with him. 'I see,' he said at last.

'I can't *help* it!' yipped Syntax.

'I know,' soothed Kane. 'I know.'

'*Golf* shoes, *golf* shoes: years and years of *golf* shoes: cleats ripping and tearing! Poor damn toes, why they never knew what hit 'em! Understand?'

'Of course. Understanding is my job.'

'It is?' puzzled Syntax. Then, 'Oh! Wait, it's, well . . . nevertheless you're . . . no. No, *yes*! That's (pause) *right*! You're a psychologist!'

'Yes, sir, I am.' Kane noticed a redness flushing the driver's neck; a twitching of the ears; back muscles tightening under a starched khaki shirt. Very little escaped his senses; they were everywhere at once. He guessed that the driver was struggling desperately to keep from laughing out loud.

Syntax's voice was the single low note of an organ playing a dirge. 'You're a very lucky man, Kane,' he mused funereally. 'Pretty *rare* in the service, Colonel, working at a job you know, uh . . . something *about*. I mean, it sometimes . . . doesn't always . . . well . . . you know, I *flew*. I was a flier!'

'You were a flier.'

'Yes, I said that. Was I . . . what? . . . or was it – Oh, no, no, no – I was a flier. Right. That's right. Then later on in my career they mixed up my . . . um . . . well – what happened . . . they put me in charge of psychological warfare. Didn't have a *clue*, Colonel, not a bloody *clue*. Why, I didn't know the psych from the (long pause) *war*!'

'Ah, but obviously you learned,' said Kane. 'With study and concentration any man of high intelligence can complete any mission. Everyone knows of your accomplishments.'

'Yes,' mused Syntax, 'my accomplishments.' He cleared his throat. 'I, uh, pioneered the principle that a five-hundred-pound sack of propaganda leaflets dropped from an altitude of, oh, say twelve thousand feet would drive a North Korean soldier roughly eight feet into the ground.'

'Very impressive,' said Kane, checking the back of the driver's neck.

'You're lying,' uttered Syntax, softly and without

malice. He sulked out the window. 'I'm a misfit. Most of us are. But we survive . . .'

Kane waited until he was sure that Syntax had finished. Satisfied, he spoke. 'Might we—?'

Syntax overrode him. '—by following one golden rule – "Don't make waves"!'

The command car halted smoothly at the iron-gated entrance to a deep-set wooded estate. An air policeman stepped smartly out of a sentry box, saluted. General Syntax returned the salute. The air policeman pressed a button and the gates whirred open. The command car beetled through and parked at the edge of the large courtyard that fronted the Slovik mansion.

Kane looked mildly puzzled. 'Here, sir? This? Is this Air Force property?'

Syntax pierced him with his stare. 'Kane, you question my leadership? Planning on writing a book?' He was sensitive on the subject. A rival British general had recently published a volume that was more than sharply critical of Syntax's planning of air strikes during World War II. Syntax, in stunning rebuttal, had dismissed it with two words. 'Jealous bastard!' The rest was silence.

'Why, no,' deferred Kane. 'Not at all, sir, not at all. But this mansion looks like—'

'Yes! Yes, it does!' interrupted the General. '*Is*! It's Bela (pause) *Slovik's* house. Modeled it after the one in all his *vampire* . . . movies. His old studio took it over and – well – uh – yes! Loaned it to, you know, to the *Air Force* – loaned it to *us* for letting us help them with that movie, that (pause) "The Longest *Night*" . . . or "Journey" . . . or something.'

'I see.'

The driver had gotten out and was hauling luggage out of the trunk. Kane stared out at the courtyard. It was empty, quiet. He mused over the gargoyles, the still-lowered drawbridge. 'Looks rather ideal for the mission,' he said. 'Peaceful – therapeutic.'

And then the sky fell down. A bugle blared. 'Assembly,' the mansion door burst open, and out into the courtyard poured the inmates of the colony: Captain Manfred Michael Cutshaw and assorted 'fail-safe' crewmen. Pell-mell, they raced, like feverish lice, all but the one named Fairbanks, who had elected to swing down on a rope that was secured to a mansion turret. He ululated shrilly like a griefstricken Tarzan searching abortively for Jane in Astoria, New York.

The inmates shoved and muddled, forming a less than military line, while Captain Groper bore down on them rapidly, a worried eye on the command car. 'Dress it up, you monkeys, dress it up!' Groper roared.

'Dress it up!' echoed Cutshaw. 'Have you men no couth at *all*?'

Groper fronted the men. 'Captain Cutshaw, shut your mouth! Fairbanks, chuck away that pigsticker!'

'Chuck my lucky *sword*?' yelped Fairbanks.

Groper quickly moosed forward, wrested the sword from Fairbanks' hand. The inmates hissed and booed him.

'Unfair!' shouted one.

'Resign!' shouted another.

Cutshaw lifted his arm at a turret. 'Get that hunchback out of the belltower; We've had *enough* hot lead on our necks!'

From the command car, Kane and Syntax watched quietly, unmoving.

'Thought-provoking, isn't it,' drawled Syntax at last.

'Yes. Indeed.'

Syntax pointed out Cutshaw. 'There's the world-famous Moon pilot.'

'The one with the golden earrings?'

'No. The one giving Groper the "arm".'

'I see.'

The driver, having stacked the luggage, now opened the door for Kane. Syntax roused himself to vigor. 'Well, my boy,' the General sparked, striving for savage good cheer, 'I wish you good luck – yes – good luck. This is out of my . . . *water*. Uh, depth – depth! But I envy you this . . . *challenge*. Yes, I do. The . . . computers say you can do it, get them . . . back on the job. We're behind you all the . . . well . . . you know.'

'Yes, sir. Thank you.'

'Laryngitis?'

'Sir?'

'Do you always talk in a whisper?'

'Yes.'

'Good! Good! Keep it! It's (pause) *soothing*!' Syntax fumbled in his pocket. 'That's . . . well . . . what did you say?'

'Not a thing, sir.'

'Good. Don't . . . well – you know . . .'

'I shall do my very best, sir.'

'Yes, yes, do. Just . . . relax and be yourself; your "Little Flower" self. Mind that nickname?'

'Not at all, sir.'

'Hard to tell if these men are batty or . . . not. Just give them tender, loving, uh, care. It'll win you your choice of new assignments.'

Some furry thought in quiet hiding gently stirred in Kane's eyes – deep, deep.

'Onward and upward!' brappled Syntax.

Kane slid out of the car, turned and saluted Syntax smartly. 'Goodby, sir.'

'Goodby. And remember – don't make waves!'

Kane turned and walked slowly to the perimeter of the wood, where he stood watching Groper severing ties with his nervous system. Syntax, in the car, mopped his brow with a deep-blue sleeve as he glanced, with naked terror, at the madly muddling men. He leaned into his driver, croaking, 'Get me the hell out of here as fast as you can!'

Kane watched, turning his head, as the car screeched away. Then he reached for a cigarette, looked to the men tormenting Groper. On his face there was no expression; it was a fixed and graven mask. But in the eyes there was movement: subtle greenish flecks spinning in a whirlpool of brown.

'Attention!' bellowed Groper. 'Dammit, attention! *Attention.*'

'I want my Ho Chi Minh decoder ring!' pouted the inmate wearing the face guard. 'I sent in the boxtops! Now where in the hell is the freaking *ring*!'

'Whoever he is behind that mask, he's a pain in the ass,' said Morris Fairbanks.

'Readyyyyyy!' shrieked Groper. '*Front!*'

The men responded. Groper called the roll.

Kane sensed a presence, someone standing near him. He calmly blew out a match and flicked it away; then slowly turned his head and saw a middle-aged captain wearing freshly starched khakis, shirt open at the neck. In his hand he gripped a stethoscope. His expression

37

dour and somber, he was staring at the inmates, sadly shaking his head. Then he turned and looked at Kane, offered his hand in friendly greeting. 'I'm Fromme – Captain Fromme. I'm the medic here at the Center. Colonel Kane, I presume?'

Kane stared at the doctor's hand and, after a fleeting hesitation, acquiesced in the breach of protocol, the lack of a salute. He shook the hand warmly, 'Pleased to meet you, Doctor Fromme.'

'Hm. Remind me to check that throat.'

Kane smiled thinly. 'It's my manner, not my throat. Don't give it a thought.'

'Suit yourself.' Fromme looked to the inmates with somber, grave compassion. 'Poor sons-of-bitches,' he murmured bleakly.

'Could you direct me to my quarters?'

'Oh, just follow the yellow brick road.'

'What?'

'Just follow the yellow brick—'

'SERGEANT FROMME, FALL IN!' bawled Groper. He was pointing to the 'doctor.'

Kane's glance flickered quickly to Groper; to Fromme; to Groper; then to a man clad only in underwear, framed in the mansion doorway.

'Damn you, Fromme, get out of my uniform!' the man in the underwear bellowed. He stomped toward Kane and Fromme like a bull with no religion.

A deadpan sergeant, crisply uniformed, popped in front of Kane, clicked his heels and smartly saluted. 'Sergeant Christian reporting for duty, sir!'

'And blasted well about *time*, Kildare!' Fromme greeted the sergeant icily. He pointed an index finger at Kane. 'Now, will you get this man into surgery or do you plan to let him stand here *bleeding* to death while you and your buddies play *soldier*! What the hell is this – a hospital or a nut house!'

Even as Fromme was concluding this thought-provoking statement, Sergeant Christian was escorting him forcibly away. The man in underwear had arrived and, passing Fromme, deftly ripped away the stethoscope; then shouted at Sergeant Christian: 'This time don't let him wrinkle the pants!' Then he turned to Kane and saluted: 'Captain Norman Fell, M.D., sir!'

In the background Kane heard Cutshaw roaring, 'Sergeant Christian, *unhand* that man!' Kane looked to the inmates as they took up Cutshaw's cry: booing, hissing and shouting together, 'Release Sergeant Fromme!'

'Gloreyoskey, Zero, let's return the salute!' Fell's speech was thick and slurred.

Kane turned and looked at him blankly. He stood weaving in his underwear, hand still crooked in salute: it was the hand that held the stethoscope. His eyes were crimson smears and he hiccupped gently, almost demurely. Kane stood motionless. 'Captain Fell, have you been drinking??'

Fell's eyebrows sickled in outrage. 'Drinking? In *uniform*?!'

After a moment of silent pondering, Kane returned the salute. 'Easy. No offense.'

'Ummm,' rumbled Fell in grudging acceptance of the apology.

'Would you show me where I nest?' asked Kane. The sudden silence behind him told him that order had been restored.

Another sergeant, heavily freckled, fronted Kane

and popped a salute. 'Sergeant Krebs reporting for duty, sir!'

'Smashed out of his mind!' murmured Fell. Kane eyed him inscrutably, then turned again to Krebs.

'Sergeant, show me to my quarters, please.'

Fell burped indignation. 'Listen, no need to ask every Tom, Dick and *Harry*, Colonel! *I'll* lead the way!' Fell drew himself erect, turned toward the mansion and husked in an undertone:

'Now, then – *march*!' He strode toward the mansion in drum-major form: head bent backward, arms swinging wide, and legs lifting high in the air.

For a moment Kane watched him; then eyed Sergeant Krebs. Krebs returned his stare – expressionless, unblinking. Then could not refrain from blurting, 'Sir, he really is the doctor!'

Kane said, 'Thank you, Sergeant Krebs.'

Krebs studied him, worried, wondering whether the comment was a subtle rebuke for insolence. He decided that it wasn't, quickly turned and followed Fell. Kane strode behind him, averting his gaze from the inmates.

'Ten – *hut*!' commanded Groper, saluting as Kane walked by the formation. Kane heard the men, in chorus, crying: 'Hail! Hail! Caesar!'

Kane stopped. He turned and looked. The inmates' arms were stiffly upraised in their wonted form of salute. Groper stood rigid, cheeks turned carmine. Kane did not move; not at all. But his eyes brushed over the men, brushed over each of them in series; and abruptly held fast on Cutshaw; on his blue, unblinking eyes staring intently into his own. Each man felt a current leaping out at him from the other; each man sensed some mystery, challenging and perilous.

Kane turned to Groper, returned his salute. 'Carry on,' he said flatly. Then walked slowly into the mansion. But at the door he paused and turned. And even at that distance, Captain Cutshaw's eyes found him. He was watching him; still watching. Kane's large and sinewy fingers gently brushed along his face, tracing a memory, an ugliness, that a Korean plastic surgeon had effaced for him years ago: a scar that had jagged like lightning from his eye to the base of his jaw.

CHAPTER FOUR

Mary Jo Mawr knew the value of time; but she spent it in the belief that someday time would return the favor. Thirty and attractive, she was a warm beach, waiting – waiting for some promise calling her name across endless hope. She knew that he would come. Although there were days when she had her doubts; days when she hated her work, hated the sun-browned laughing girls who were always young while they were with her and usually married when they left. She was resident dean of women at the Consuelo Endicott College for Girls. Now she walked along its corridors whiffing chalk and perfumed cashmere.

'Oh, Miss Mawr?'

Mawr eyed the senior who had fallen in step with her, a honey-haired lisper named Sloop. Clydene Sloop. She wore braces on her teeth and clearly needed them for her head, which was largely stuffed with the lurid contents of unexpurgated editions. She slunk.

'May I be excused from gym?' wheedled Sloop.

'No,' drawled Mawr in her laconic Vassar pucker. 'You may not. You need to lose weight.' It was one of those days when she hated sunsets.

'My, I think I'm rather svelte,' gritted Sloop.

'I think you are rather fat, Miss Sloop, and I'll not endure any insolence.'

'*Insolence*?'

'Insolence. An inevitable derivative of overweening pride.' Clydene was the daughter of the Secretary of

43

Defense. And she damn well knows it, thought Miss Mawr with a splash of venom. She halted abruptly, putting her hand on the knob of a door that was marked *'Founder.'* 'Onward to gym, Miss Sloop,' she ordered, adding, 'Fight Fiercely, Endicott!' Then pushing open the door, she glided into the Founder's office.

'Snot!' breathed Clydene. Then jiggled down the corridor with yards of slink to spare.

'Miss Mawr, Miss Mawr, what now, what now? What are we at, eh? What? What's the game, what's the—? Whoop! Here, now, where are my glasses? Where, where, where? Where have I put them?' Miss Consuelo Endicott sent fumbling pink fingers crackling through papers on her desk while Miss Mawr eased into a chair, flipping her hair back from her eyes. Mawr's nostrils twitched inquiringly as the Founder recovered her glasses, putting them on with delicate care. Mawr had her suspicions but had never been quite sure: Scotch or bourbon, she couldn't tell which; breath is such a *personal* thing.

'Now, then, Miss Mawr.' The Founder's hands were clasped studiously under a still beautiful face; still beautiful at fifty, even with dissipation. She dyed her hair, Mawr knew well; but, why not, she thought, why not? Maybe *she* was waiting, too. 'Precisely what is it you wished to see me about?'

'I believe you sent for *me*. The inmates?'

'Inmates?' The Founder's eyes glazed over, gave her the look of a cocker spaniel who has just seen St. Francis in a Park Avenue penthouse. Then she belched unequivocally, snapping her eyes into focus. 'Yes, the *inmates*!' she declared. 'The inmates. Of course.' Once

44

more she fumbled through papers, knocking an ornamental Buddha and an ashtray to the floor. At last, flushed and triumphant, like Venus hotly rising, she came up with the sought for document. As prepared by Miss Mawr, it was a typewritten list of grievances adumbrating, at length, certain acts of classic outrage that had been perpetrated against the school by the madcap inmates of a mysterious United States Air Force installation which, as had already been vividly demonstrated, was literally but a stone's throw away and set apart only by a wall.

The lofty turrets of the mansion commanded a conqueror's view of the school, so that among the list of charges were such stunning provocations as:

(A) the hurling into the library window of two stunned frogs, an insulted and outraged bullfinch and a lox and cream cheese sandwich, the means of propulsion being a crossbow and there being appended to the payload an enigmatic printed note that stated simply: 'POLICE BRUTALITY.'

(B) the parachuting of a snake onto the girls' volleyball court, the appended note reading, this time: 'LOVE ME, LOVE MY ADDER.'

(C) the loud and choral chanting of all but the last line of various obscene limericks during 'Parents' Day' ceremonies, a phenomenon artfully capped by a sudden barrage of flying jockstraps during the serving of tea on the lawn. The inmates had also posted a sign, discernable from the lawn, on a mansion turret, reading: 'Consuelo Endicott has crabs!'

(D) numerous telephone calls to resident members of the school staff during the dead of night, with only heavy breathing heard from the other end of the line, although once a voice reportedly said, 'Repent!' While on still another occasion the anonymous caller stated simply, 'Varicose veins!' and promptly hung up.

(E) heavy mailings to the staff of Rosicrucian literature, a wondrously inscrutable venture that was followed, hard upon, by the arrival on the campus of proselytizing ambassadors of Jehovah's Witnesses, Mendicants for Christ, the Coptic Orthodox Church, the Fifteenth Church of Christ Cyclotron, a local Baptist church and one bewildered Millerite. All of them claimed to be there at the request of Miss Endicott and were difficult to dispose of, especially the Witnesses, who had come equipped with a phonograph and records, and had obstinately refused to leave until the records were horribly smashed by a sturdy Miss Klutz, who taught the girls at the school gymnastics and happened to be a Catholic.

There had been more, much more. 'Innumerable acts of audacity too numerous to enumerate,' as Miss Mawr had once expressed it. Mawr had put it to the Founder and asked that she deal with it, knowing that it was hopeless. The Founder dealt with nothing. She was content with having founded. For six full days she had labored, and now was fixed, like a moth in jade, in an endless seventh day; perpetually resting, The rest she left to Mawr and to Mawr's various predecessors.

'Oh dear, oh dear,' sighed Miss Endicott, smoothing the rumpled list as she fidgeted like a blue jay waiting its turn to attack Alfred Hitchcock. 'These charges, Miss Mawr . . .'

'What shall we do, Madame Founder?'

'Do? Yes, *do*. What shall we *ever*, ever do!'

46

'I thought you'd decided, Madame Founder. -I thought that was why you'd sent for me.'

'Yes, of *course* I sent for you.'

'Yes.'

'What are "crabs"?'

The silence that ensued had an airless, lunar quality; and through the window, from the tennis court, floated a faint and faraway cry that sounded like 'Score.'

'They are vermin,' said Miss Mawr.

'Vermin?'

'Vermin. Parasitic vermin.'

'Not salty things that scuttle?'

'No,' said Mawr, expressionless. ' "Crab" is a slang expression.'

'Oh. Well, that's what I thought. Yes, I – well – of course. How could anyone have a *crab*?'

'They can't,' Mawr said soberly, fighting down a giggle.

'Then why do they say I have them?'

Mawr grew vaguely uncomfortable. 'The expression wasn't meant literally. It is slang for a tiny bug.'

'Bug?'

'Bug.'

'Is it something like the "clap"?'

Miss Mawr nearly fell off her chair. 'Something.'

'Should have said so in the first place.'

'Well, I—'

'Damn bloody nonsense,' the Founder grumbled testily as she pulled open a drawer and reached for something in it – then recollected something – possibly Mawr's presence – and quickly slid it shut again. She blinked across at her dean. 'What was that you said?'

47

'Not a .thing, Madame Founder. But what shall we do about the—?'

'Nothing. Nothing at all, my dear. It's all been taken care of.'

'Oh?'

'Taken care of,' the Founder repeated sagely. Her hand had pulled open the drawer again and suddenly she seemed rather anxious to be rid of Miss Mawr. 'The trouble,' she rattled brusquely, 'was that foolish Colonel Ryan. I'm *convinced* that he was the trouble. He was naughty to those men; very naughty, very cruel; ran that place like a snake pit. Did you ever see that movie?'

'No, I—'

'Ran it like a snake pit, hiss-hiss-hiss! Don't concern yourself, my dear. No. Not at all. Sufficient unto the day.'

Mawr waited for her to continue before she realized that the Founder had concluded her remarks. 'How' – she probed with delicacy – 'has it all been taken care of?'

'What?'

'The incidents. The inmates next door.'

'Oh. *That*. A new commanding officer. Arrived there today.'

'Oh, I see.'

'Yes. You see?'

'Did he call?' asked Mawr.

'What?'

'The new commander. Is that how you got the news?'

The startled, fleeting shadow of something like panic flitted vaguely, for an instant, across the Founder's face. 'Yes!' she said quickly. 'Yes, the dear

48

heart called. Said that everything would be – fine!'

'Good show,' drawled Miss Mawr. Then excused herself and left. For a moment she paused outside the door, her head bowed in thought. Muffled and indistinct, she heard the opening of a drawer, the clinking of glass; and smiled in bemusement. The Founder was just like her father, she thought: her gentle, beery father who used to drink on the sly to repel the Boston chill. But then, what could one do with a banker who read John Donne aloud? Except love him, she thought; love him; that's all.

A chattering of girls tinkled lightly down the corridor and vanished around a corner. Mawr moved to a window, looked out across the campus to the wall; and then above it to a turret of the gruesome Slovik mansion.

She blinked; then blinked again. The inmates had posted a new banner: *Mary Poppins has Syphilis.'*

CHAPTER FIVE

Captain Norman Fell gently tipped the grinning skull atop the skeleton in his office so that the vodka bottle inset in its base could pour its contents through its gaping oral cavity into a coffee cup in his hand. 'Don't blame *me*!' he admonished the skull. 'I *told* them not to operate! Remember? Eh?' The skull did not remember, splashed vodka onto his fingers. Fell gently licked them. He bore the skull no malice. Yet there was in him something dangerous.

Fell's clinic reeked of defiance. Against one of its walls rode a white-sheeted medical examination table on over-sized wagon wheels, and set against the head of it stood a high and smugly venerable Dickensian accountant's stool. On the walls, in heavy crayon, bold red arrows pointed to jars containing *'Aspirin!' 'Band-Aids!' 'Dental-Floss!'* and *'Lemon Drops!'* Another pointed out a *'Suggestion Box'*; and above them all a master inscription, crayoned in green, proclaimed: *'Self Service.'* Gaudy and squat and pouting heavily in a corner crouched a pinball machine that Fell had repainted so that its highbacked electric scoreboard now read: *'Light up the Interns and Win a Free Game!'* Fell thought it grand.

Humming inanely, Fell tucked a folder under his arm and moved to the clinic door. He was still in his shorts, above them an open-necked, blue wool shirt. He stepped outside into the Slovik main hall.

Like the exterior of the mansion, it was Gothic, massive and dense, with a high cathedral ceiling crisscrossed by beams from some enchanted, moaning wood. This was the Therapy Room for the inmates, cluttered with lounge chairs, chess sets, ping-pong tables, stereo, motion picture screen and projector; writing tables, magazines and canvases, set on easels, vivid with paintings by the inmates. No painting was quite completed. Each was a tale of horror abruptly halted in mid-narration. One was of an index finger that pointed straight up and was pierced by a needle, dripping blood. Another depicted a tree, its terminal branches metamorphosed into the coils of a boa constrictor crushing the head of a male infant; its creator had captioned it 'Mother Love.' Still others were infinitely busy and chaotically detailed, yet with fine-drawn precision so that in a single painting one could identify a jackhammer, part of an arm and an onrushing train; the wheels of a lathe, a baleful eye, a Negro Christ, a bloody ax, a bullet in flight and a creature half-lizard, half-man. From the center of one billowed a hydrogen mushroom cloud, while high, high above it, almost microscopic in size, hung a silvery bomber pierced by a spear; on the fuselarge, in red, were the tiny letters, 'Me.'

Fell glanced around the hall. It was quiet and deserted. He looked to the winding staircase that ascended to the second floor, where all the staff were billeted. No one on the landing. He looked around the hall again, at the fixed and myriad lifelike effigies of the old master vampire, of Bela Slovik as he'd appeared in his various movie roles. Then shivered slightly, walked down the hall, pushed open the door to Kane's office and stepped inside.

The new commanding officer was unpacking some books. His back was to Fell, but as the door slid open silently, he turned with the cunning grace of a middle-aged panther. Eyes like a panther as well, thought Fell, and closed the door behind him. He strode over to Kane, who had a hand in a valise that was open on his desk. Above the desk, in matching frames, were portraits of Slovik and General Lastrade, posed in attitudes suggesting that they were no longer speaking.

'Hi,' chirped Fell thickly. 'Brought you a little present.' He tossed the folder onto the desk. 'File on Manfred Cutshaw. Better read it, old shoe.'

Kane eyed him inscrutably. 'Do you intend to get dressed?'

'Well, now, how can I get dressed when Sergeant Fromme won't surrender my *pants!*' growled Fell, projecting wounded innocence. 'Colonel, you surely don't expect me to *rip* them off!'

'No, no – of course. We mustn't use force.'

'We mustn't wrinkle the *pants!*' Fell slurped noisily from his cup and abruptly subsided. 'He'll take them off neatly soon as Cutshaw gives the order.'

'As soon as *Cutshaw* gives the order!'

Fell's eye fell inadvertently on a book in Kane's valise. It was a Roman Catholic missal. For only the briefest instant he pondered its implications; then looked up again at Kane.

'May I give you some advice?' said Fell as he made an abortive effort to sit gracefully on the edge of the desk. He slipped, barely recovered, then pretended

53

that nothing had happened as Kane looked to his coffee mug, then up again at the medic.

'Get Cutshaw to like you,' imparted Fell with heavy wisdom. 'Humor him. Pamper him. The inmates won't *listen* to anyone else. Get Cutshaw on your side and you've really got it made. But get him on your back and you can kiss the game good—'

Fell never finished. The door flew open with the suddenness of a horrible realization, banged with a crash against the wall. In bounced Cutshaw like a jack-in-the-box, a pixie on springs. 'It is I – Manfred Cutshaw!' he announced with sparkling grandeur; then slammed the door behind him and marched up to Kane, fronting his new commander with a challenging posture, arms akimbo. 'So – you're the "new boy"!'

Kane sat on the desk edge. His gaze never left Cutshaw's as his hand reached for his file. 'Yes,' he answered mildly. 'I'm Colonel Hudson Kane.'

'Do I call you Hud?'

'Why not call me Colonel?'

'Why not call you Shirley MacLaine! Why are we quibbling? You're on the way *out*! I've been deputized to inform you that we refuse to be led by a sissy!' Cutshaw's gaze flicked over at Fell. 'Captain Fell,' he demanded severely, 'are those *my* jockey shorts?'

'Friend,' intervened Kane, 'by whom were you deputized?'

'Angels and archangels! Cherubim and seraphim! Unseen forces too numerous to enumerate!' Cutshaw boldly snatched the file from out of Kane's grasp, flipped it open to page one and then thrust it rudely back at him. 'There! It's all in the file! Read the file, the file, the file!' His finger stabbed at a paragraph. 'There, Colonel, there! Under "Mysterious Voices"! You think Joan of Arc was crazy? Well, you're bloody well out of your mind! She had acutely sensitive hearing, Hud! Like me, your adorable astronaut! The file, Hud, read it! Read the file! Read the file!'

Kane glanced down at the page.

'Out *loud*, out *loud*! It's part of my therapy!'

Fell had moved to a window where he watched the two men silently. Kane looked to him and he nodded. 'Very well,' said Kane. 'Sit down.'

Cutshaw sat. Putting an arm around Kane's neck, he leaped nimbly onto his lap. And froze; waiting; staring deep into Kane's eyes.

Kane's expression was unreadable. 'On a chair,' he said softly.

Cutshaw glided swiftly into a chair by the desk, assuming there a posture much like that of Rodin's *Thinker*, staring intently and unblinkingly up at Kane. Fell hicupped gently.

Kane began to read: 'Captain Manfred Cutshaw . . .'

'Dammit stop that whispering!' Cutshaw interrupted. 'Do it *right*! Do it *right*! It's supposed to sound *massive*!' Then, 'Mannnnnfred Cutshaw!' he demonstrated stentorianly.

Kane raised his voice. 'Mannnnnnnnfred Cutshaw . . .'

'Beautiful! Beautiful! Go on! Go on!'

Cutshaw silently formed the words with his lips as Kane read aloud: '. . . Two days prior to a scheduled space shot, subject officer Cutshaw, while dining on base, was observed to pick up a plastic catsup bottle, squeeze a thin red line across his throat, and then stagger and fall heavily across a table then occupied by the Director of the National Space Administration, gurgling, "Don't order the swordfish!" . . .'

Then ensued a silence for several beats while Kane ingested this information, staring dully at the file. Then he continued with his reading: 'On the following afternoon, subject officer quite uncharacteristically knocked a gas station manager into extended insensibility when the latter refused to deduct a cost equivalent in lieu of trading stamps. Later the same day, subject officer suggested to his commanding general that he "shave off his mustache" because it looked "silly". In his general remarks at the time, subject officer also alluded to his "firm and unshakable opinion" that "people with weak chins should not attempt to con a foolish but trusting public".' Kane could not refrain from looking up. 'Did you *really* say—?'

Kane halted in mid-sentence, startled by what he saw: a white mouse crawling up the astronaut's shirt front. Cutshaw's hand flew up to a medal that hung from his neck. 'You're looking at my medal!' he snapped. 'Stop looking at my medal!'

'I'm not.'

'Yes, you are! You covet it!'

Kane looked down at the file. Once more he began to read: 'On the following . . .'

'Isn't it beautiful?'

Kane again looked up. Cutshaw was holding his medal, fondly admiring it, head bent over. It looked to Kane like St. Christopher. 'Yes,' said Kane, 'it is.'

'There, I *knew* it;' raged Cutshaw. 'You were *looking* at it!'

'No.'

'Yes, you *were*!'

'Then, I'm sorry.'

'*Sure*, you're sorry!' fumed the astronaut. 'What good is "sorry"? The damage is *done*, you envious swine! How can I *eat*! How can I *sleep*! I'll be a quivering, nervous wreck waiting for you to make your move! For a kleptomaniac colonel to come padding up to my bedside and rip away my medal!'

'If I were to try something like that you would awaken,' reasoned Kane.

Cutshaw would have none of it. 'Powerful drugs,' he gritted, 'could be insinuated into my soup. You could—' Kane, he suddenly noticed, was staring at the mouse. 'Aha! You want the *mouse*! Here, Hud, take him! Leave me the medal!'

'I do not want the mouse *or* the medal,' said Kane.

'Who the hell offered them?' Cutshaw rebutted, smoothly pocketing the mouse. 'Now read! And eat your heart out!'

Kane's eyes brushed over him, then returned to the dossier. 'The following morning at—'

'Your hands are very large,' interrupted the astronaut.

The comment drew Fell's attention to the Colonel's hands. Yes, noted the medic; they *are* rather large.

'I know,' said Kane mildly.

'Congratulations!' rasped Cutshaw. 'Now spare me the interruptions and get on with my therapy. I haven't got all day. There are *mice* to be fed!'

Kane resumed his reading: 'The following morning at 0500, subject officer entered his space capsule, but on receiving instructions from Control to begin his countdown, was heard instead to say, "I am sick unto the death of being *used*!" While being carried out of the capsule, subject officer plainly announced that if "nominated" he "would not run, and if elected would not serve". He later expressed his "profound conviction" that going to the Moon was "naughty, not suave", and in any case bad for his skin. Political affiliation: Anarchist; professes to hate officers . . .' Here, Kane looked up, puzzlement prowling his eyebrows. 'Cutshaw, *you* are an officer.'

'That's all very well for *you* to say; you're *sane*!' responded Cutshaw.

'Aren't *you*?' parried Kane.

'If I were, would I still be sitting here playing "Youth Wants To Know" with a pansy?'

Fell slurped from his coffee mug, staring at Kane's back with a physician's eye; at his hands clenching the desk edge. The 'Little Flower', he judged, had rather powerful muscles, and they presently seemed to be operating under some sort of massive restraint.

'Why,' tempered Kane, 'do you hate officers, son?'

'Why do camels have humps and snakes not? Don't ask the heart for reasons, Hud!' Cutshaw leaped up. 'Just pack up and leave!'

'Why won't you go to the Moon?'

Cutshaw sat down again like a flash. 'So you're staying!'

'Yes, I'm staying.'

Cutshaw leaned forward portentously. 'Schmucks dance after dinner; sheiks sleep,' he intoned; then leaned back.

'Meaning what?'

'How do *I* know? The *voices* told me to say that!'

'Cutshaw—'

'Wait! Wait-wait-wait!' The astronaut's hand flew to his brow as his eyes pressed tightly shut in thought. 'I'm getting a message for – "H.A."! Is there an "H.A." here with us tonight?'

'No,' sighed Kane and *'Wrong!'* pounced Cutshaw. '"Horse's Ass" will do quite nicely.' Then with a 'Shhhh!' – waving Kane to silence – he closed his eyes in groping frown again. 'Attila! It's Attila the Hun! Wants to know if you'll accept the charges!'

'What is the message?'

'He want a ball of "Silly Putty" and a "Batman Is a Fag" sticker.'

'Why won't you go to the Moon?'

Cutshaw leaped up. 'What's *there*?' he demanded. 'Viet without Nam? What's *there*? What's *there*?'

Kane looked thoughtful. 'When Columbus sailed from Spain, did he dream he'd find America?'

'Columbus was an idiot! Starts out looking for India, winds up in Pismo Beach! Honestly, Hud, I'm starting to *worry* about you!'

The door flew open, banging against a wall.

'Doctor Fell, I need attention.'

The inmate in the beret stood framed in the doorway. In one hand he held a palette, in the other a brush, and in his mouth a Greek accent.

Fell weaved toward him. 'Blue Cross? Blue Shield? What's your coverage?'

'Coverage?' the inmate looked fuddled.

Kane intervened. 'What is ailing you, my boy?'

'Who but Douglas! *Always* Douglas!'

59

'Lieutenant Douglas Morris Fairbanks, the one with the sword,' explained Fell.

The beret quivered with outrage. 'Once *again* he has given me that fiendish "Mark of Fairbanks"! *Look!*' he pouted, turning. 'I am bleeding!'

He wasn't. But slashed into his trouser seat was a very palpable '*F*'.

'Only a scratch,' said Fell. 'Get a band-aid from the clinic, Corfu.'

But Corfu was eying Kane, vexed by some problem of weight. 'You are Colonel Kane?' he asked.

'Yes. I am.'

Corfu rubbed his paint brush into the palette. 'Your coloring is bad.'

'Look out!' cried Fell; but much too late. In a sudden, lightning movement, Corfu had brushed red paint onto both of Kane's cheeks.

'There!' Corfu beamed. 'Not a "Portrait of Jenny", but at least not Dorian *Gray!*' He raised his paint brush high in salute. '*Ciao!*' he grinned, and left.

A desk drawer slammed shut. Kane whipped his head around, saw the astronaut tossing a folder onto his desk, declaring, 'I'm ready.'

'Ready for what?' queried Kane.

'For the ink-blot test. It absolutely flips me!'

Kane, thought Fell, looked slightly apprehensive.

Kane spoke flatly, 'Ink-blot test?'

'Yes-yes-*yes!*' bubbled the astronaut. '*Now*, while you're *fresh* with those *roses* in your cheeks!' Kane wiped his face with a handkerchief. 'Come on, let's go!' continued Cutshaw. 'You're a *psychologist*, right?'

Kane threw a darting glance at Fell. Then quickly

looked back at Cutshaw. 'Very well – we'll do just one. And then the rest when I've fully unpacked.'

'No, the *batch*!' Cutshaw sulked. 'I want the *batch*! The bloody *lot*!' He scraped his chair to the side of the desk. 'Hud, I swear, I'll be good for a week!'

Kane saw Fell staring out the window: humming; dreaming; swishing the contents of the mug. 'All right,' said Kane. 'All right.'

Kane sat behind the desk, opened the folder – he'd brought it with him – to the first of a series of Rorschachs. Cutshaw bent his head over it, his nose almost touching the page. He studied the blot intently. Then he looked up at Kane. 'Well?' he demanded.

'Well, what?' responded Kane.

'Well, ask me what I *see*.'

'What do you see?'

'An elephant on water skis.'

'Right. Now this one.' Kane turned the page. Fell stared into his coffee mug, then turned to regard the Colonel with a mild look of amazement.

Cutshaw examined – for barely a moment – the second of the Rorschachs, then firmly announced his judgment: 'An old lady in funny clothes blowing poisoned darts at a buffalo.'

'Right. Right again,' said Kane.

Cutshaw looked into his eyes. 'You're purely out of your *mind*, Hud! You're purely full of *shit*!'

'If you say so.'

'Ingratiating bastard. You're insane, but I adore you.'

'Good.'

'Watch your tongue!'

Captain Fell had moved in closer. 'Listen,' he began, 'aren't Rorschachs supposed to be—'

'Later we'll do the rest,' Kane interrupted very firmly. He closed the folder with finality, shoving it back into the drawer.

'Marvey!' glipped Cutshaw, leaping bolt upright.

'And now you'll be good for a week?'

'No!'

'Cutshaw, didn't you tell me that—?'

'Yes! Yes, I did! But I'm an incorrigible liar!' Cutshaw swept to the door, crouched over like Groucho Marx, and flung it open with a bang. 'May I go?' he asked urbanely.

A corporal in uniform, capped in the hat of a chef, stood revealed in the doorway, his hand gripping a ladle that brimmed with a murky substance. 'Colonel, you've got to taste this!' he burbled, stepping inside.

With a swift, birdlike motion, Cutshaw lowered his nose to the ladle, then jerked his head up at Kane, announcing: 'Truffles from the Moon, Hud! Dusty, but good for your sex life!' He swept out of view.

The corporal advanced on Kane, the ladle prowed forward. 'Taste it!' he said. 'Taste it! I just made it up!'

Kane eyed him levelly over the ladle. 'What is it?'

'I'm not sure,' retorted the corporal. 'Take a taste, take a taste!'

Kane slurped a taste. The corporal, rather corpulent, jiggled him stomach up and down. 'Tell me!' he demanded. 'Tell me, tell me, tell me!'

'And to whom am I speaking?' asked Kane.

'Corporal Gower.'

'You're the chef?'

'How did you guess?'

Kane smiled thinly. 'Just a shot in the dark. I think your stew is tasty.'

'Great!' exulted Gower. 'We'll have it for dinner!' He jiggled out of the office, gracefully tossing onto the floor, in an absent-minded reflex, the steaming contents of the ladle.

Fell watched the sinews in the psychologist's neck as Kane stared down at the splotch the stew had made on the floor. Cutshaw appeared at the door, examined the splotch with concentration. 'A lobster eating Johnson grass!' he decided, and crouched away.

Fell closed the door, dropping some newspaper over the splotch. 'The cook, by the way, is not an inmate,' he explained. Then he wandered to a bookshelf, examining its new contents.

Kane poked aimlessly at a corner of the newspaper with the point of his shoe. He spoke as though to himself. 'We all defeat madness in various ways.'

Fell quietly waited. But Kane said no more.

The medic pulled a book from the shelf. 'This yours? Elementary psych?'

The psychologist looked up at him. 'Yes. Yes it is.'

Fell flipped through the book, noted some marginal glosses as well as some very heavy underlinings. 'You're a lucky boy, Kane,' he said: 'assigned to a job you do best.'

'Aren't you? You're a doctor.'

'Brain surgeon.'

'Oh.' Kane moved to his desk, calmly resuming unpacking.

'I am *stunned*,' declared Fell, 'by your shock and amazement.'

Kane's hand was on the missal. He stared at it solemnly. 'We're all miscast – one way or another. Being born into this world: that's the ultimate miscasting.' He paused and seemed to be brooding over what he had just said, feeling for his thoughts with gentle, surgical fingers. 'I – think that's what drives us mad. I mean – if fish could survive – actually *survive* out of water – they would go mad.' Kane looked up at Fell. 'Do you know what I mean?'

'No. But maybe I'm drunk.'

Kane picked up the missal, sat down behind the desk. He put the missal into a drawer and slid it shut; then uttered softly: 'Haven't you ever had the feeling that we – weren't meant for this place?'

'Well, I go where the Air Force sends me.'

Kane shifted his leg, heard a loud and anguished 'Yip!' as a disreputable-looking spotted mongrel dog scrambled out from under the desk. The office door was flung open.

'So *there* you are!' pounced a large-nosed, elfish inmate, pointing imperiously at the dog.

'Lieutenant Leslie Spoor,' explained Fell.

Kane stood up. 'Is that your dog?' he asked mildly.

'Does he look like my *zebra*? What's the *matter* with you, *any*way!' The dog licked Kane's shoe. 'Look,' said Spoor, 'he likes you!'

'What do you call him?' asked Kane.

'Irresponsible!' answered Spoor. 'He's ten minutes late for rehearsal! Now *out*!' he commanded the dog. It padded meekly through the door and disappeared, and in the background Kane saw Fairbanks throwing a leg over the second-floor balustrade and sliding down the drape.

Fell cleared his throat. 'Lieutenant, the Colonel would like to hear about your work.'

Spoor shriveled him with a glance. 'Navigating? Child's play! I leave it to the crows, to the hawks, to the swallows! I am not a mere *device*! I am not an albino *bat*! Watch your cup, dear heart, it's dripping.'

'Not navigating,' said Fell. 'Your *work* – tell the Colonel.'

'Ah! You speak of matters tender!'

'Lieutenant Spoor,' explained Fell, 'is currently at work adapting Shakespeare's plays for dogs.'

Spoor drew up proudly. 'A massive problem! A labor of love! But it must be done! It must! It must!'

'Of course,' soothed Kane. 'You taught Shakespeare in civilian life?'

'I repossessed cars for a finance company.'

'Highly commendable,' diplomatized Kane.

'A *joy*!' exclaimed Spoor. 'Man versus Machine! Leslie Marvin Spoor against the criminally poor! A battle of wits! A clash by night! Will .007 recover Fu Manchu's Lotus? Will he? Will he? I *loved* it, sir, I *loved* it! What are you driving?'

'I'm using a staff car,' said Kane.

'Paid for?'

'No,' intervened Fell. 'Now tell the good Colonel what you're rehearsing.'

'*Julius Caesar!*' crackled Spoor, fixing Kane with a glittering eye. 'It's that terribly gripping scene where this noble-looking Dalmatian whips his toga about him – *thus* – and pitifully snarls at one of the conspirators: "*Et tu, White Fang!*"'

The ensuing silence ticked like a bomb as neither Fell nor the Colonel moved. The broad grin of triumph slowly faded from Spoor's face. At last he said, 'You hate it.'

'Not at all,' Kane answered quickly. 'I'm just thinking about it.'

'Good! We'll discuss more fully later. In fact, I'd very much like your notions on a problem I'm having with *Hamlet*. What a puzzler! See? If I cast a Great Dane they'll accuse me of—'

The dog barked urgently outside the office door. Spoor held up a hand, palm outward, to the Colonel. 'The time is out of joint,' he mourned and glided to the door. 'Julius awaits! He awaits! Later, Colonel Pussycat! Anon! Anon!' He swooped out the door, then, and disappeared from sight, his voice calling, 'Coming! *Coming*, Rip Torn!'

Cutshaw appeared in the doorway, tossed a pair of pants at Fell. 'Here,' declaimed the astronaut. 'Fromme has just decided that he will sell all his goods and give the proceeds to the poor.' Then he glowered at Kane. 'Still with us, Colonel Kidd?'

The crash of a hammer pounding plaster resounded through the wall. Cutshaw looked to the side. 'Ah, that darling Captain Bemish!' he said. Then oozed out of sight.

Again the crash of the hammer. Through the doorway Kane saw Groper racing swiftly down the stairs. He looked to Fell, but the medic had turned his back and was gazing out the window, humming a song from *Rose Marie*. Kane went to the door, looked to the right and saw Bemish. He wore his crash helmet and face guard and was sedulously pounding a hole into the wall outside Kane's office with a short-handled sledge hammer.

Groper ran up to Bemish and ripped the hammer from his hand, yapping, 'I *hid* it, dammit, I *hid* it! How did you get it, Bemish? *How*?'

'I wouldn't *dare* tell you *that*,' said Bemish. 'Mighty Manfred would *kill* me!' Then he whipped the hammer deftly out of Captain Groper's grasp and instructed him, serenely, to 'Kindly stand aside.'

'You little—!'

Groper had lifted his arm as though to strike at Captain Bemish, and, at this, Kane intervened. 'Captain Groper, I am shocked – *shocked* at your behavior!'

'But he's—!'

'Later we can discuss it, Captain. But presently, you're dismissed.'

'Listen—!'

Groper was about to say more, but he abruptly severed the flow as his eyes looked into Kane's. Something stirring in them chilled him. He felt an inexplicable terror that no logic could dismiss. He took a step backward, stiffly saluted, and quickly retreated to his quarters.

Kane watched him go, then put an arm around Bemish's shoulder. 'Now, then, tell me, Captain Bemish: why do you do that to the wall?'

Over the Captain's shoulder, far down the hall, Kane caught a glimpse of Cutshaw staring intently through a crack in the dormitory door. When Kane caught his eye, the door closed quickly. Kane looked back at Bemish. 'You were saying?'

'I was saying?'

'The wall, Captain – tell me.'

'What's to tell? What's to tell? I mean, to a man of

67

your intelligence; a psychologist, a colonel, and goodness knows what *else*.'

'Goodness knows. Now just tell me.'

'Well, the spaces,' said Bemish intensely.

'Spaces?'

'Yes, the spaces – the empty spaces between the
atoms in my body – or *your* body, if I may get personal – may I?'

'The wall.'

'Yes, the *wall*, Colonel, the *wall*! What in the hell
do you think I'm *talking* about?'

'The wall.'

'That is correct. Now, then, kindly pay attention.
See, the spaces between the atoms – I mean, relative to
their size – are *immense*, simply *immense*! It's like the
distance, frankly speaking, between Earth and the
planet Mars! And do you know what the distance *is*?'

'Immense.'

'You are wise beyond belief.'

Colonel Kane glanced at his watch. 'About the
wall . . .'

'Look, the atoms won't *leave*! They are not going
*any*where! Relax!'

'But—'

'Atoms can be *smashed*; they cannot *fly*! Not a
chance! They're only—!' A notion occurred to Bemish. 'Oh! Listen, wait! You have to go "toy-toy"?'

'No, I don't.'

'Then what's the hurry? Now those same empty
spaces – *immense* empty spaces – between the atoms in
your body – *your* body, mind you – well, those spaces
also exist between the atoms in that *wall*. So walking
through the wall is simply a matter of gearing the

holes – of gearing the holes between the atoms in your *body* to the holes between the atoms in that *wall* – that naughty, stubborn *wall!*' Bemish punctuated his statement with another swing of his hammer. Plaster crickled in cloudlets to the floor and Bemish looked sullen. 'Nothing,' he muttered. 'Nothing.'

Kane said, 'Why do you strike the wall?'

Beamish mustered fresh attack. 'I keep experimenting, see? I concentrate hard. I try to exert the force of my mind on the atoms in my body so they'll mix and rearrange; so they'll fit just *exactly* those spaces in the *wall*. And then I try the experiment – I try to walk through the wall. I just took a running *bash* – and I failed – horribly.'

He swung once more at the wall and another hole gaped forth. Both he and Kane stared silently at what he had just done. Then at last Kane spoke. 'Why did you do that?'

Bemish whipped his head around and scruted Kane piercingly. 'My Colonel, do you mock?'

'Not at all.'

'Very good of you.'

'Why did you strike the wall?'

'I am punishing the atoms! I am making of them an example! An object lesson! A *thing!* So when the other's see what's *coming* – when they see I'm not kidding *around* – why, they'll fall into *line!* They'll let me pass *through!*'

'May I?' asked Kane, lifting the hammer ever so gently from Bemish's grasp.

'Sure!' agreed Bemish. 'Swing! Enjoy! Maybe they'll *listen* to a stranger!'

'I had something else in mind.'

Bemish looked outraged, grabbed for the hammer; gave first a tug; then a mighty pull. The hammer failed to move a fraction from Kane's apparently effortless grip. Bemish looked at the hammer, then at Kane, slightly fuddled. 'Your grip is strong, "Little Flower".'

'I think,' said Kane, 'that your problem may lie in the properties of the hammer. Some nuclear imbalance. May I keep it awhile for study?'

'Are you possibly putting me on, sir?'

'Not at all,' said Kane, 'not at all. Why don't we discuss it again tomorrow?'

Bemish left him, muttering, and Kane returned to his office, where he found Fell atop his desk, bare legs folded like a Hindu fakir. He was staring into his coffee mug, mumbling incoherently, then looked up, startled and annoyed, as Kane dropped the hammer on the desk. 'Would you care to put on your trousers?' asked Kane.

'I was just sitting here sort of thinking about it.'

'Your trousers?'

'Anything, Colonel; anything to keep my mind off . . .' His words trailed off into inner space. Then he roused himself abruptly. 'What do you think of Bemish?' he asked.

Kane eyed him levelly. 'He's a very sick man. What *else* am I to think?'

'Maybe,' muttered Fell.

'Maybe?'

'Maybe. He's probably putting us on. They're probably *all* putting us on. Hell – isn't that why they're here? Why they're not in padded cells? I mean, examining psychiatrists—'

'Did not create the world,' finished Kane. His words were edged in frost. 'Have you ever lived with danger, Fell?'

'No.'

'Well, neither have I. But what about riding to "fail-safe" point with your fanny sitting over enough atomic juice to melt New York? What about it? Day after day, week after week. And never ever sure that maybe *this* time you go beyond – *this* time, maybe, you *drop* it. Well, maybe they're kidding us, Captain; maybe it's all a con. Rest assured I intend to find out. But I know this much – *this* much: these men were the best the Air Force had. Most are highly intelligent; most are many times decorated; and Cutshaw, Manfred Cutshaw, holds the Congressional Medal of Honor. So I find it rather difficult to believe that they're all goofing off.'

Fell slid off the desk, started squirming into his pants. 'Hydrogen nerves, fine,' he said. 'That explains all the "fail-safe" crewmen. But what about Cutshaw? What about *him*?'

Kane stared thoughtfully down at the newspaper still spread over the splotch of stew. 'Cutshaw is something else,' he brooded; 'something very – mysterious. And "madness in great ones must not unwatched go." '

Fell snapped his belt buckle in with a click. 'Life,' he muttered cryptically, 'is just chock *full* of mysteries.' Then he looked up full at Kane. And left without further comment.

Kane resumed his unpacking. Only once was he interrupted, and that was when Cutshaw appeared at his

71

door to ask simply, 'Why do animals suffer?' and then promptly melted away.

At three that afternoon, Kane began dipping into summaries and histories of the men. Spoor and Fairbanks had been navigators; Bemish a bombardier; Corfu a pilot; and Fromme, radioman-gunner. Still another, a Lieutenant Dorian Zook, had been a pilot with an especially distinguished record. Kane interrupted his reading for a snack: milk and a cheese sandwich. Then he resumed his studies voraciously. At five, Cutshaw returned, bursting into the office and slamming the door behind him.

'Still here?' demanded Cutshaw.

'Yes,' said Kane. 'Sit down.' Then added quickly, 'On a chair!'

Cutshaw ignored the offer. His glance skimmed the titles of books freshly placed on the office shelves. 'So! It is true!' he snapped with vigor. 'You are not Colonel Ryan in some clever new disguise!'

'Disguise?'

'Yes, disguise. Once he returned to us in the skin of a caribou. But we recognized him instanter. Know what we did to him, then, that lout? Kane, we gave him the "silent treatment." Hell, we wouldn't even *nod* to him. Insolent, antlered bastard! He finally went away. You are not Colonel Ryan.'

'How do you know?' asked Kane.

'Your books. Colonel Ryan read *Reader's Digest*. You read Thomas a Kempis. Why? Why do you read a Kempis? Are you a Catholic?'

'Yes, I am.'

'Tough shit.' Cutshaw swooped to Kane's desk,

slamming his medal onto mahogany. 'Here! Here's the medal! You've got what you came for! Now get lost!'

Kane thoughtfully fingered the medal. 'St. Christopher,' he murmured.

'And what were you expecting, Hud – St. Caribou of the Cross?'

'Your records,' commented Kane, 'make no mention of religion. Have you any affiliation?'

'Indeed, indeed!' said Manfred Cutshaw. 'I am a Flaming Knight Rampant of the Christian Hussars! Now ask me what we believe in.'

'What do you believe in?'

'That colonels consort with elks. Now get out of here, Hud; I'm losing patience with you swiftly.'

'So,' said Kane, 'you'd like me to go.'

Cutshaw suddenly seized his wrist. 'Are you *mad*?' he cried emotionally. 'And lose the only friend I've *got*? Oh, God, don't do it, Hud, don't do it; Don't leave me alone in this house of horrors!' His grip was like the talons of a terrified hawk. Kane gently twisted free.

'Sit down,' said Kane. 'Let's talk.'

'Yes!' shrieked Cutshaw like a Fury finding a hair in her dry martini. 'I want to talk! I want therapy! I want therapy this instant!' He dove to a couch against the wall, turned on his back and stared up at the ceiling. 'I'd like to tell you about my boyhood and all that kind of crap.'

'Free associate,' said Kane.

Cutshaw turned and eyed him severely. Then leaped off the couch, crouched to the desk, recovered his medal and returned to the couch. Then said nothing for over a minute.

'Well?'

'I'm collecting my thoughts, Hud! Shut up and think about grass!'

Kane waited.

'I was born,' began the astronaut, 'in Jackson Heights, New York.'

'Your records say Brooklyn.'

Cutshaw sat up angrily. 'Listen,' he shouted, '*I'll* sit over there, okay, and *you* come lie on the couch and we'll see how well *you* do! What are you, a smartass?!'

'Forgive me. Go ahead.'

Cutshaw resumed the position. 'Okay,' he said. 'Okay, I wasn't born at all. I was launched at Cape Kennedy. The Russians recovered me and delivered me to my mother: Maude – Maude Cutshaw. Then some creep from the Immigration Office told her I was an alien. She thought he meant a Martian and clobbered him with a bedpan. She was mean, at times, but cuddly. Not like my father. Groper was just plain mean.'

'Groper?'

'Captain Groper.'

'Captain Groper was your father?'

'I was his illegitimate son. I also had three illegitimate sisters named Ugly, Vulgar and Tawdry. That's when Pop was a movie critic for *Time* magazine. Things were good in those days, Hud; profoundly, rippingly good. Pop was a real "in" thing. Yeah. Luce used to call him an oracle. Sure. Pop said a picture stunk and people would *run* to see it. I swear, he never missed. Except once, for about four months, when some

74

counter-oracles in Hollywood started making these flicks about teen-agers surfing and giving them foreign-film titles like "Mondo Surf" or "Katzman, Mon Amour". Pop used to look at the cast list – he never *saw* the movies – and see Annette Funicello and maybe Troy Donafoop. Then he'd grit his whole body. Drove him *crazy*; out of his *mind*! Couldn't make a decision. But he finally went with the titles; gave them all a rave. The public liked them *any*way. And that's when he started drinking. I always could tell when he was smashed because he'd start to talk in captions. Like, "After the melon, a grape". Or, "Back of the crisis, a grunion". He'd also say "brouhaha". Whenever he said "brouhaha" Moms would swat him in the chops with a rolled-up copy of *Newsweek*. It was the closest he ever came to being in contact with the facts.' Cutshaw turned his head and eyed Kane slyly. 'Do you believe any of this horseshit?'

'No.'

'Just testing.' Cutshaw stared again at the ceiling and began to speak rapidly, barely pausing for breath. 'When I was a kid I used to play horseshoes . . . Horseshoes are like life. I don't know exactly *how*, but I feel certain there's a connection. Had lots of friends who played horseshoes, but mostly they tortured caterpillars. Cut them up and burned them. Also cut the tails off dogs. Know why they did it? Because they were bastards. Yeah. And, Hud, they grow *up* to be bastards. That sheriff in Alabama who clubbed a lady demonstrator while two of his duddies held her down? Lynch mobs? Eichmanns? The ghouls who gather at accidents? who slow their bloody cars down on a freeway to see the wreck? Same —— bastards, Hud; they

just grew up; that's all. Show me a kid who kills caterpillars, and I'll show you a son-of-a-bitch. Let some kid
put a hand on my mouse and I promise I'd castrate him
instanter and save the world from more of him. Hud,
I trust you approve. I dearly crave approval. I dearly
need approval. I would rather have approval than a
jelly roll with yoghurt. Now my father, Captain
Groper, hell, he's *steeped* in the blood of caterpillars.
Notice he never takes showers? No, you only just got
here. But you'll notice, Hud, you'll notice. He never
takes a shower; we'd see the green all over his legs.
Not a pretty sight, love, not a pretty sight at all. Hud,
I'd rather be *dead* than green! But he's my father;
what can I do? Get up a petition with ten thousand
signatures and have him deported to Argentina? What
can you *do* with the useless bastard! Hud, once he re-
viewed a stag film and said that it was "dull". Then
after all the commotion started he actually looked at
the films. It destroyed him, Hud, destroyed him. That's
what made him join the Air Force. He was a major
once, you know. Yeah – Major Groper. Then he
happened to say "brouhaha" in front of a brigadier
general and they busted him back to captain. Ah,
enough of this maudlin chatter, Hud. And stay awake,
you monster, I'm not spilling my guts for *laughs*!'

'I'm awake.'

'You were nodding, Catherine Earnshaw!'

'I assure you,' said Kane. 'I was not.'

'You are *determined* to start an argument! But as
usual I'll give ground. I'll accept your sniveling per-
jury. Hud, what's happened to Scarlett O'Hara? What
has happened to gracious living? Tell me, what do you
think of asps?'

'Asps?'

'You are absolutely incapable of giving a straight answer!'

Kane blinked. 'I didn't follow the question.'

'You couldn't even follow the spoor of the Incredible Colossal Man. How do you get to the *bathroom*, Hud? How do you ever *find* it! Your uniform looks clean but I doubt some foul play.' Cutshaw produced a lollypop and began to lick at it noisily.

'Earlier,' said Kane, 'you came to my door and asked a question. You said, "Why do animals suffer?"'

'Yes.'

'Cutshaw, what did you mean?'

'What did I *say*?'

'You said, "Why do animals suffer?"'

'Then that's what I *meant*, you blazing ass! What do colonels get a month, Hud? I'm writing a letter to Congress!'

'Cutshaw, why did you ask the question?'

'Impertinent, saucy bastard. I asked you what colonels *got*. Now don't play Socrates with Cutshaw, friend! Whose therapy *is* this?'

'Certainly not mine.'

'Do you believe in God?'

'Yes.'

'What kind of a Catholic are *you*?'

Kane raised an eyebrow. 'I'm confused,' he said.

'Ah! The beginning of wisdom!'

'Are you a Catholic?'

'Never mind *that*, you oaf! Ask me about my obsessions!'

'Will you answer?'

'Yes. I will.'

77

'Very well,' said Colonel Kane. 'What are your obsessions?'

'Well, frankly, I hate feet.'

'The way they smell?'

'The way they *look*. Hud, I cannot stand the *sight* of them!'

'Does that include your own?' asked Kane.

'*Especially* my own! How could a wise and beautiful God give us ugly things like *feet*! Give us *padding* things like feet! They're a disgrace! An anomaly! A *disaster* area, Hud! If God exists he is a fink!'

'A fink.'

'Or a foot. Yes, a foot. An omniscient, omnipotent *Foot*! Do you think that is blasphemous?'

'Yes,' said Kane, 'I do.'

'I believe I capitalized the "F".'

'I believe you're referring to the problem of evil.'

'I am referring to the problem of *feet*! Christ, don't complicate the argument; it's tawdry enough already!'

'Let's go back to animal suffering.'

'No, let's not,' said the astronaut, making a clearly abortive effort to wrap a leg around his neck.

'But isn't it all the same thing? What you're saying about feet? Namely, how can there be evil coexistent with a good God?'

'Hud, kindly stick to feet.'

'You think they are ugly.'

'I *know* they are ugly.'

'But without them how could you walk?'

'Good *Foot*, you are dumb! Give me *wings* so I can *fly*!'

'Ahh,' breathed Kane, leaning back in his chair. 'So

we've come to the heart of the matter. At last we've come to flying.'

Cutshaw leaped up out of the sofa and Grouchoed to the door. 'Want my opinion, Colonel Caribou? You are a quack nonpareil!' He opened the door, swooped outside and disappeared from Kane's sight.

Kane clasped his hands under his chin and began to ponder. Fell looked in. 'How's it coming?' asked the medic.

'Is Cutshaw Catholic?'

'I'm not sure. I think he was. Yeah, maybe he was.'

'That seems to figure,' murmured Kane.

'Why do you ask?' inquired Fell.

'It seems to be very much on his mind. Perhaps it's related to his problem.'

'The latest con,' mumbled Fell.

'What?'

'Nothing. See you around the campus.'' Fell quietly closed the door.

Kane returned to his study of the men's dossiers. When that was completed, he went to the bookshelf, plucked out the elementary psychology text that Fell had noticed earlier. Kane opened it to the bookmark and immediately was immersed in very deep study. Now and again he would underline. At times he would flap open a dictionary and look up a word.

The inmates' dormitory was neatly lined with footlockers, cots and washbasins. In a corner of the massive room a fireplace blazed with flame, logs crackling merrily. The inmates were gathered around Cutshaw.

'What's the plan?' asked the one named Zook. He was a wiry and dark-complexioned man, and had eyes that probed like death rays, deep-set and close together.

'We'll start with "D",' responded Cutshaw. ' "Acts of insolence much too insolent to be recognized as insolence." Then from there we go to letters and from—'

'Wait a minute, *wait* a minute,' Corfu interrupted. 'Why are we trying to get rid of him? The man seems very gentle; not at *all* like Colonel Ryan.'

Cutshaw pinned him with scorn. 'He is also a psychologist – a very *top* psychologist. He *knows* too much, you horse's nose!'

'I like him,' said Corfu.

Cutshaw eyed him for a moment, and his expression, it seemed to Corfu, spoke of a tugging inner conflict. Then Cutshaw returned to Zook. 'Are you ready, my little star?'

'No,' said Lieutenant Dorian Zook. 'What's my motivation?'

'Fear,' said Cutshaw, 'fear. Stark, staring fright. This boy Kane is Foxy Grandma, Zook, the type that's really dangerous. Plays it dumb right up to his teeth. So keep your guard up every second!'

That evening Kane met Zook. His eyes red from study, the new commanding officer was ascending to his quarters when the former pilot approached him.

'You!' rasped Zook.

Kane halted, blinked his eyes. 'What do you want?' he asked wearily.

'*Wrong!*' stabbed Zook.

'I'll ask you again – what do you want?'

Zook bowed his head, mopped his brow with a sleeve and muttered, 'Boy, oh, boy – *another* one!'

Kane looked down at his shoes. 'I'm your new commanding officer. I am Colonel Hudson—'

Zook interrupted fiercely, spewing, '*Listen*, baby, I *know* who you are! Now why play "Let's Pretend"!'

'What do you mean?' asked Kane, looking up, suddenly alert. 'Pretend what?'

'That you can't read my thoughts! That we're not on the planet Venus and that *you're* not a *Venusian*! That you haven't invaded my mind to make me believe I'm still on Earth! Now come off it, sweetheart; it's all hypnotic illusion! I'm not on Earth and you're not an Earthman! We're knee-deep in *fungus* and *you're* a giant *brain*! Now don't give me stories; just give me back my *flying* belt!'

'Flying belt?' Kane echoed.

'Fying belt?' mocked Zook, pitching his voice to an insulting falsetto. 'Maybe you're *not* a brain at *all*. You could be a giant *parakeet*!'

Kane tried edging past him. 'Later, why don't we—?'

Zook blocked his passage, his voice loud and demanding. 'My Buck Rogers flying belt! I want you to give it back!'

Kane smiled bleakly. 'Oh, I see. So you can fly?'

'Why do you *think* I want it, dum-dum! So I can play Tinker Bell in *Peter Pan*? Listen, straighten out your tentacles, baby, I'm *worried* about you.'

'So am I,' muttered Kane.

'Oh, is that a Venusian wisecrack? Beautiful, kid; that's all I need – elephant jokes from a bug-eyed monster!'

'Look—' tempered Kane.

But Zook began to bellow. 'You've *got* my space ship, you've *got* my zap gun, you've *got* my body – what more do you *want*! Why do you want my *belt*?'

Kane, desperate for sleep, made another futile

attempt to get past him. 'I don't *have* your belt,' he insisted. 'And I'm really not a Venusian.'

Zook's tone was humoring. 'Sure, baby, sure. You're an Earthman. Swell. Now who won the ball game?'

'Today?'

'*Wrong*!' Zook leaned his head in close to Kane's conspiratorially. 'Level with me, sweetheart: are you just one brain or two glued together? I mean, glued kind of sloppy-like, 'cause kid, I've got to be honest with you: sometimes I ask you questions and you don't *answer* me too good.'

Captain Groper appeared before them. 'Sir?' he said to Kane. 'Do you still want Captain Fell?' Shortly before, Kane had asked to see him.

'Yes,' said Kane; 'yes.'

'Well, he hasn't checked off the grounds,' said Groper, 'but we can't seem to find him anywhere.'

'*Sure*, you can't find him anywhere!' bawled Zook. 'He's flying around with my *belt*! *Get him down*!'

Like some Air Force genie out of a wild blue lamp, Sergeant Krebs appeared magically, and in one liquid motion hustled Zook away from Kane and in the direction of the dorm. 'Get him down!' roared Zook, in the fierce grip of Krebs. 'Get him down or I'll burn all your fungus! You hear? You hear? Your saucers, I'll break all your saucers, you'll be grounded just like me! I've had about all that I can stand, you brains! Wait until I tell them! When the Interplanetary Council hears that—!'

A door slam cut him off. Kane heaved a sigh and looked to Captain Groper. 'Not in his room?'

'I knocked. But no answer. And it's locked. This happens pretty often, sir. Just seems to disappear.'

'I'll see him in the morning.'

Groper seemed verging on making a comment; but withheld it, moved on. Kane put a hand on the banister, then noticed that Corfu was slapping brush onto canvas in the center of the hall. He hummed as he grandly dabbed. Kane squinted to make out the painting. Then saw it well enough. It was a purple, winged foot arching majestically under a halo.

CHAPTER SIX

Alice Hesburgh, the Senator's wife, had a sultry, roving eye with the memory of a camera when it came to one fact: Once, at Michigan State, she'd been Sweetheart of Sigma Chi. It was there that she'd met the Senator, then a lecturer in government. He was fifteen years her senior, but she thought he looked 'wise'. The Senator, for his part, thought she looked preternaturally sexy. She unearthed for him dreams of lust that he had long ago misplaced.

Their dates had been surreptitious, but at last, when they were discovered, the rumor spread like crabgrass that sweet little Alice was diligently trading her body for the promise of passing grades.

The scandal was squelched by their engagement, but in the wake of the announcement came a flurry of dark murmurings among the male undergraduates. They were threatening to lynch Hesburgh for 'crimes against fraternities' and 'the practice of demonology.' One burly junior, a tackle on the football team and clearly enamored of Alice, was ready to swear under oath that he'd seen Hesburgh 'in a wizard's cap drawing a pentangle around Alice while talking white mice danced around him in trance.' This bizarre threat, however, came to no fruit. Nor did the pleadings of Alice's mother that she was 'mesmerized by an Electra complex,' the argument melting to ashes in the face of Alice's reminder that she'd never *seen* her father, who had hied himself to the wilds of Tierra del Fuego with a lady softball player just three days after Alice's birth.

Alice married Hesburgh.

They were settled now in Georgetown in a house along the Potomac near the university campus. Hesburgh was now forty-five and Alice merely thirty. She could pass for less and frequently did. On moonlit nights when the fusty Senator was deep in filibuster, Alice would slip into tennis shoes and a shaggy, oversized sweater and import her sizzling charms into a local campus beer hall. At times she attended football rallies, and once, in an incredible extension of her thought-provoking activities, was nominated for 'Homecoming Queen' by a campus club at Georgetown. The Senator only discovered it when a request came to his secretary for some 'eight-by-ten glossies' of Alice. Their life was not serene.

Alice was not a homemaker. For example, the Senator's milk bills ran to ninety dollars per month, a rather compelling figure when one considers that they were childless. Alice would open a bottle of milk, pour out a cupful, and leave the bottle uncapped on a table, where inevitably it soured. She also loved to redecorate, room after room and over and over again: from Modern to Japanese to Provincial to Early Tudor to whatever struck her fancy. Whenever the Senator balked, she would scream about Medicare, which Hesburgh staunchly opposed. 'Old folks are dying,' she would shrill, 'and all you can think about is milk . . . that and Chinese Modern!' He could never find proper rebuttal. He saved it for the Senate floor, where he would lacerate waste in government with a fury that left him hoarse.

Yet it was jealousy that moved him most mightily,

even drove him into inanities. Once, in his bedroom (Early Mandarin that month), after discovering that Alice had been given the lead in the senior class play, he dared to threaten her with a letter opener (Persian, left over from July), husking in wild, bathetic tones, 'If I can't have you, *no* one will!' He was prevented from further idiocy by the entrance of the maid bringing Alice a glass of hot milk.

The two of them were standing now in the National Gallery of Art in Washington, D.C. The bronze head of a boy, pulled dripping from the Aegean where countless years of lying on ocean bottom had turned it a flaky green, now stared out at them with lustrous eyes that gave it a look of life. Hesburgh, intent, was spelling aloud from a guidebook: 'E-p-h-e-b-e – Ephebe. Ephebe of—'

Alice interrupted him, nervously twirling a glove. 'Oh, never mind, darling; it's really such a bore.'

Hesburgh pursed his lips, glaring up from the guidebook into the eyes of the Ephebe. 'It's a classic work of art,' he gritted.

'Hm?' throated Alice, automatically primping her hair as she spied an attractive male some yards away in front of a Picasso. He'd caught her eye and now he wafted her a quite innocent smile. 'What was that you said, my dear?'

'I'm trying to build an image, fairest. Now please don't make any waves.' Suddenly Hesburgh saw the man, saw Alice still staring.

'Oh, what a perfectly *marvelous* "peace dove,"' she cooed, starting to move away. 'I think I'll wander over—'

'Back!' Hesburgh grabbed her arm and held her. 'It's a ringtailed hawk!'

'Oh, *honestly*!' whined Alice. 'Nolan, people are watching!'

As Hesburgh looked to see who might be watching, she escaped. Simultaneously, a burly man in uniform backed into him, his nose deep in a brochure. Both men turned.

'Oh, pardon *me*,' said the man in uniform, 'I was—' He stopped and stared at the Senator. It was General Lastrade. He made an elephantine attempt at feigning surprise at the encounter. 'Why, Senator *Hesburgh*!' he clucked. 'I never *dreamed* you were an art lover!'

The Senator's eyebrows gathered like the dark clouds of a storm. 'And *I* never dreamed that you wore crepe-soled *shoes*! You lightning-billed egret! What the hell do you *mean* creeping up on me here in a hallowed hall of culture! I will *hear no special pleading for your bomber appropriation!*'

'You do me *wrong*, sir, *wrong*!' The expression on Lastrade's face was an example of outraged innocence.

Hesburgh was about to retort but he suddenly spied Alice chatting gaily with the man whom she'd been ogling the moment before. 'Alice!' he barked sternly, and hastened toward his wife.

Lastrade looked deep into the eyes of the Ephebe and grunted, 'I blew it!'

The Ephebe made no reply, a phenomenon to which it owed its continued survival as an integral work of art.

CHAPTER SEVEN

Captain Groper knew the difference between himself and a Persian rug. The bane of his life was simply that others had never recognized the distinction. Am I a zoom? a cup of pudding? he would ask his pillow every night until he grew surfeited with the answer, which was never the one he wanted. Fresh out of high school, he'd sold insurance, rising to dizzying heights of obscurity capped by the day when his boss clapped his back and told him, 'Groper – you're okay.' Then Groper read T. E. Lawrence, somehow connected it to Beau Geste, which he read six times within a week. Soon after that he joined the Air Force in the vague and visionary hope that they would assign him to find the 'Blue Water', and that when he'd found it, the world would find him. But from the beginning he'd been an adjutant, a crisply uniformed in-basket; still a Persian rug. Cutshaw was not a rug, he knew, nor any of the other inmates. He hated them for that.

He sat in his office, reading poetry when the call came from Miss Mawr. She would not speak to him, however; that was his Karma; he'd expected it. She wanted Colonel Kane. Groper decided that it sounded urgent and went seeking his commander.

Ten pensive days had passed at the mansion. Colonel Kane had left instructions that he was not to be disturbed except in case of an emergency, then locked himself in his quarters. During his retreat the Slovik mansion gave off an air of fretting restlessness, of being

89

at loose ends, shifting on its foundations from haunch to massive haunch, waiting for Kane to emerge. Cutshaw had pounded on his door several times, but got no answer. He seemed rueful and chagrined, and, after the third day, slightly frantic. He took to writing messages on useless scraps of paper and then slipping them under Kane's door. One of the messages stated that *'Tawdry Groper eats unblessed venison!'* Another issued the challenge, *'I can prove there is a foot!'* And still a third made the comment that *'There is nothing less attractive than a caribou that pouts!'*

Kane never made an answer. And Cutshaw grew more frantic. Once he stood outside Kane's door wailing, 'Heeeeeeeeeeaaaaaaathcliiiiiiiiiifffff!' over and over for half an hour. By the seventh day he was maddened and plunged headlong into action that he felt sure would flush Kane out.

And now, three days later, the astronaut smiled with satisfaction as he watched from a mansion window while Kane drove off to the Endicott School.

Miss Mawr was arranging her desk when Colonel Kane knocked at her door. 'Do come in,' she drawled laconically. Kane entered, removed his hat.

'Miss Mawr?'

Mawr looked up at him, looked into his eyes; and suddenly felt that she was drowning, roaring down Niagara like a twisting, pummeled log in the grip of wild, unthinkable power.

'Miss Mawr?'

Was he the one?

'Miss Mawr!'

Slowly she surfaced, took a breath and tried to float. She also removed her glasses. '*Awfully* good of you to come, Colonel. Please; please sit down.' She gestured to a chair beside her desk and Kane slid into it.

'Your phone call sounded urgent,' he said.

'Well, yes – yes, it was. Now I know you're busy so I'll get right to it. Uh, these grounds, as you may know, were once part of the Slovik estate.'

'Yes.'

'I really can't imagine why he sold to Mrs. Endicott; he was still at the top, you know. But the fact is that he did, Colonel, and that makes us neighbors.' She motioned out the window. 'Nothing but that wall to keep our twain from ever meeting. And that is the problem, Colonel Kane.'

'What do you mean?'

How strong yet mild-mannered, she thought; almost deferential. She brushed back her hair and twirled her glasses, striving for coolth and firmness. 'Well, the school is rather posh, you know; girls of high breeding and all that sort of thing. You'll understand it, then, if I ask you, sir, to keep your men in bounds?'

Kane looked puzzled. 'In bounds? You mean they're climbing over the wall?'

'What a thrilling idea, Colonel. But the wall is much too high, I fear, and your men are far more cunning. There's a fiendish mind at work over there. Now, my frankness may sound deplorable, but really, we've all had quite enough.'

'Enough of *what*, Miss Mawr?'

'Enough of *this*, Colonel Kane!' She plucked an envelope from her desk and officiously extracted a letter. 'I received it this morning. May I quote?'

'Please do.'

'Good show!' reacted Mawr. She hesitated a

moment, then decided to don her glasses. It was absolutely essential; she couldn't read without them. She picked up the letter and began: ' "To my darling, my dearest, my flaming secret love! How I've hungered for this moment when I might rip away the mask and unburden my bleeding heart! I saw you but a moment – an instant – *semi*-instant – yet I knew I was your slave! There could be no other love, not for me, not forever! Wondrous creature, I adore you! You are sandalwood from Nineveh, truffles from the Moon! In my dreams I am a madman! I rip away your dress, and then your slip and then your glasses and I—" ' Mawr looked up at Kane. 'Well,' she said; 'etcetera.'

'What's the point?' inquired Kane.

'Did you write it?'

'Did I *what*?'

Mawr spilled the thimble of hope that she had been clutching against all reason. 'No, I really didn't think so,' she sighed. 'But for one mad moment I *did* get a quiver.' She extended the letter to Kane. 'The signature – see it?'

Kane saw it clearly. It read 'Colonel Hudson Kane.'

'The author is a master of surprise,' added Mawr. She slid the envelope across to him. 'Here, take a look.'

Kane examined the envelope. The address was dully printed on a serrated sticker and bore all the earmarks of a mass commercial mailing. Nowhere in the address did Miss Mawr's name appear. It was directed simply to '*Occupant.*'

Cutshaw was busier than a hummingbird in June. A sheaf of letters in his hand, he was padding up and down among the inmates in the dorm. They were hunched over footlockers, scribbling, brooding, thoughtfully biting the ends of ballpoint pens. Suddenly Cutshaw swooped upon Zook, flicked an eye over what he was writing. 'Slashing, Zook, slashing!' he said, then lifted his head to the others. 'Gentlemen, Zook has come up with "throbbing pulse" and I think we should all try to use it!'

Corfu, nearby, lifted a pondering look to Cutshaw. 'Bestial lust?' he inquired tentatively.

The astronaut beamed with pleasure. '*Splendid, Corfu!*' Then he loudly commanded the inmates to 'add "bestial lust" to the list of basic phrases.'

An inmate named Nammack fronted Cutshaw with a letter. 'Do I give it to Fromme?'

'Heavens, *no!* I must *grade* it!' Cutshaw whipped the letter away, turning now to Klenk, a quondam pilot, who, at the moment, looked inspired. Meantime, Fromme was at a typewriter, busily typing addresses onto stickers under carbon paper, thus achieving an effect that was not dissimilar to an addressograph machine. He used a telephone book as his source, selecting the names of hapless females that were prefixed by a 'Miss.'

Klenk blossomed, 'Finished!', lifting his pen with a flourish.

'Marvey good!' commended Cutshaw. 'Sign it "Colonel Hudson Kane"!'

Cutshaw glided over to Fromme, now humming 'Some Enchanted Evening' while his finger skimmed hopefully down a page in the phone book, halting at last at one that pleased him. 'Miss Vorpal Katz,' he announced. 'Now she's *got* to be a loser! Right?'

'Right!' Cutshaw was rapidly flipping through the

letters he had collected. He halted at one, chagrined, and looked up with fury at the men. 'Okay, fellas, who signed "Lamont Cranston"?'

Fairbanks was upon him, thrusting a letter into his hands, burbling, 'Here! It's a classic! Does the best one get a prize?'

'Douglas, *heaven* will reward you. Tomorrow night some lonely spinster will be pressing your words to her lips. Doesn't that make your juices tingle?'

'I think we should have some kind of incentive.'

'Douglas Morris, I just *gave* you one.'

'Bah!'

'What?'

'Your incentive reeks of socialism. Freaking *creeping* socialism.'

Cutshaw had glanced at Fairbank's letter, and now thrust it back at him with annoyance. 'Do it over! "D" in spelling!'

Fairbanks' hand flew to his sword. The astronaut lifted an eyebrow. '"F" in deportment. You'd draw your sword on Mighty Manfred?'

'I am merely holding the hilt.'

'I interpret it as a threat.'

'Can't a man hold his hilt?'

'That is a quibble.'

'For heaven's *sake*, who's *quibbling*? I am merely holding my *hilt*!'

A breathless Spoor had burst into the dormitory and now irrupted between them. 'Mighty Manfred, I saw it again!'

'Saw *what* again?'

'The Lady in Black! The Phantom of the Nut

House! How the hell do I know! I swear it, it looked like a ghost! It had *three giant heads!*'

An exasperated exhale fluttered out of the astronaut. 'Never con a con man, Spoor; never fox a fox.'

'But I *saw* it! I really *saw* it!'

'Then you're *crazy*, really *crazy!*'

It was conceded among the inmates that Lieutenant Leslie Spoor entertained magnificent obsessions. For instance, once he had reported that while strolling through the grounds on a cloudless, moonlit night he'd heard 'hissing from above' and, looking up, detected Groper 'crouched in the branches of a cypress, deep in whispered conversation with a black-and-white owl.' Nothing had shaken him from this story. When the astronaut gently admonished him that the estate was visibly barren of any variety of cypress tree, Spoor had eyed him pityingly and very softly rebutted that 'anyone with money can pull out a tree.' He had further advised that 'certain parties then could easily fill in the hole.' And 'Groper,' he'd added triumphantly, 'is still *here!* Notice?'

From that day forward, no one noticed Spoor; or, especially, his persistent sightings of a certain 'Lady in Black' whom he claimed was prowling the Slovik grounds – 'twice on Shrove Tuesday!' There was only one way to be rid of Spoor, and Cutshaw now adopted it: he quickly walked away from him, heading for the door. And walked into the arms of Groper.

'Come with me!' growled the Captain, seizing the astronaut by the shoulder and hustling him into Kane's office. 'Here he is, sir!' he gruffed, shoving Cutshaw through the door.

Kane, seated at his desk, held up the letter addressed to *Occupant*. 'Did you write it?'

'Are we going to have a scene, Hud?'

'Kindly answer the question.'

'But the question is pre*post*erous!'

'The handwriting, though, is *yours*.'

Cutshaw snatched up the letter and quickly crumpled it in his fist. 'Fap! A crude and obvious forgery!' He tossed the letter over his shoulder and kicked it in mid-air.

'Good,' said Kane; 'good. That being the case, you won't be annoyed.'

'At what?'

'That letters addressed to *Occupant* will henceforth not be forwarded but ceremonially burned.'

'I protest!' cawed the astronaut.

'Then you *wrote* it!' pounced Kane.

Cutshaw leaned across the desk. 'Oh, you're a psychological devil, Hud! I'm putty in your hands! *Yes! I wrote the letter!*'

'Got him!' grinned Groper.

Cutshaw spread-eagled his arms in a sacrificial gesture and in the process managed to 'accidentally' cuff Groper's face. 'Shoot me for giving the spinster hope! Love to the loveless! Depravity to the deprived! Never mind the space race, Hud! Feed me to giant ants! Yes! Make widows of five hundred pen pals!'

'Purely a pleasure,' breathed Groper.

Cutshaw leaned in closer to Kane, and lowered his voice to a whisper. 'Sir, I've noticed an exotic odor in here, and being as you're a colonel, sir, it's got to be Captain—'

Groper moved in to him menacingly and Cutshaw

leaped behind Kane, shouting, 'Don't let him touch me! I'm *crazy*!'

Kane stood up, lowered his head and ran a hand over his eyes. Cutshaw shook him roughly as he eyed a menacing Groper. 'Stay awake!' he rumbled at Kane. 'I may need you, Colonel Caribou!'

The room suddenly trembled with the vibration from a hammer blow. Groper turned pale orange. 'Where did he *get* it!' he fumed, then turned hooded eyes on Cutshaw. 'Did *you* give him the hammer?'

'Listen, is this going to be like the strawberries, Queeg? If it is I'm having no part of it!'

'Captain Groper,' Kane said softly, 'kindly handle that disturbance.'

Groper saluted and went out after Bemish. Cutshaw still clung to Kane. 'Colonel Caribou, you were grand,' he said.

'Thank you. Please let go.'

'Is it safe?'

'Perfectly safe.'

Cutshaw patted Kane's head. 'Bless your nostrils, Hud, you're marvey. Now let's talk.'

'What about?'

'Where the hell have you *been* for the last ten days!'

'In my room.'

'Doing *what*?'

Kane said, 'Reading.'

Cutshaw said, 'Hah!' then brazenly ripped the Colonel's shirtsleeve from the wrist all the way to the shoulders and fell to scrutinizing his arm.

'What are you doing?' said Kane, expressionlessly.

'Looking for needle-holes, you idiot. Show me a Catholic and I'll show you a "junky." A kindly old

97

teacher told me that, a Baptist minister named Farrago. Told me that monks have frolics with nuns.' He rolled down Kane's sleeve. 'You're clean. Sit down.'

Kane sat on the couch and Cutshaw raced swiftly back of his desk, plumping heavily into the chair. 'Now talk! *Talk*, you monster; spill your guts out.'

'Didn't you ask to talk to *me*?' said Kane.

Cutshaw pounded the desk, roaring, 'Silence when you're speaking to me! And cover your feet, sir, they offend me!'

'Feet or Foot?'

'Are you awake?'

'Of course,' said Hudson Kane.

'And you really believe in Foot?'

'Yes.'

'Blind faith?'

'Faith; not blind.'

'The terms are mutually exclusive, ass.'

'There are arguments from reason,' said Kane.

'There are arguments from reason,' snapped Cutshaw, 'for baking people in ovens! Do better than *that*, Colonel Aquinas!'

'Give me a moment and I'll try.'

'Fap!'

'For life to appear on Earth,' began Kane, 'a protein molecule of a certain configuration was the necessary building block. Hundreds of *millions* of them, in fact, but just for the moment, assume it was one.'

Cutshaw yawned elaborately, looking at his watch.

Kane ignored it, kept talking. 'For just one of these molecules to appear by chance would require a material volume of more than sextillion, sextillion times that of the known size of the universe. And considered strictly from the angle of time, given a material volume the size of the Earth, such a probability would require – well, guess how many years?'

Cutshaw glared and answered, 'Ten to the two hundred forty-third power *billions* . . . That would give us just one molecule of the right configuration: but in fact, for life, we'd need billions! Right?'

Kane looked stunned. 'Right.'

'And all that proves,' thrust Cutshaw, 'is that we read the same books.' He rose. 'Colonel Aquinas, do me a favor.'

'What?'

'Pack up and leave; you're an insufferable bore!'

The astronaut Grouchoed out of the office, slamming the door behind him. Kane exhaled heavily. Then got up, stooped to the floor, picked up the crumpled letter to Mawr. He stared at it a moment. Then abruptly, blindly, he threw it against the wall. It struck the portrait of Lastrade.

Kane opened his door and stepped into the hall. He saw Groper in a far alcove, grappling with Bemish for the hammer. Kane walked slowly toward the staircase, then paused to examine the inmates' paintings, looking to find some new addition. He did find one in bright, fresh colors. It was a Pop Art sketch of Smilin' Jack. The cartoon hero was depicted plunging a rapier into a blubbering 'Fat Stuff' who was hiding behind a weather map in an airport control tower. It was captioned rather simply: 'How, now! A rat!' And was unsigned.

'May I speak to you for a moment?'

Kane turned, saw Fromme. 'What is it?'

'I want schooling, sir, schooling. I wish to fulfill my

life's ambition. I can't live without my dream, sir. It's been my dream since I was a boy. It isn't too late if I go to school.'

'Medical school?'

'Don't be absurd. I wish to play the violin. I wish to play "Humoresque". On a stage,' added Fromme.

'Come to my office tomorrow morning,' said Kane. 'We'll talk about it then.' He walked to the staircase and Fromme called after him, 'Get some sun and eat fresh fruit!'

Kane went to his quarters. But as his hand took hold of the doorknob, he quickly turned his head to the side. He thought he had seen, peripherally, the long trailing folds of a black velvet gown disappearing around a corner near the far end of the landing. For once he doubted his senses, but investigated anyway. As he was about to turn the corner, he heard the closing, soft, of a door. He rounded the corner. Now he stood in the East Wing. No one was quartered there but Fell. He went to his door – knocked – no answer. He waited a moment, then returned to his room; never heard Fell growl behind his locked door: 'Where the hell have you been!'

During this time, Lieutenant Spoor had entered Kane's office in search of his dog. He found him, as he'd suspected he would, crouching under the desk and plainly reluctant to emerge. Spoor tugged at his collar, pulled him whimpering across the carpet, chiding, 'Rip Torn, you are incorrigible. It's a *play*, just a *play*! Clown, the knives are made of *rubber*! See? You really don't get killed! It's only—!'

Inadvertently, Spoor saw a book propped on a shelf beside the door. 'Look! Hey, look! Colonel Kane!

He reads the Bard!' Spoor rushed to the shelf and pulled out the book while a grateful Rip Torn raced back to the desk. '*Madness In Hamlet!*' glowed Spoor. Then, 'What is this fad for long titles,' he grumbled. 'The old one was good enough. Contemporary, contemporary; everything's got to be "in".' He avidly thumbed through the first few pages.

Kane had no sooner entered his room when a shriek of searing, white-hot pain ripped into his brain. Involuntarily he gasped, clutched at his head and fell on his bed. For moments he writhed. Then the pain slowly subsided; but it left behind its footprints: a pounding steady ache. Locked in his office were the pills that brought Kane ease. He had only five left. He lurched to his feet and started downstairs.

From the staircase Kane saw chaos. Lieutenant Bemish clung to a drape approximately eight feet off the ground while Captain Groper hurled threats from below. Bemish still had the hammer and announced unequivocally his yearning to drop it on Groper's head 'in the interest of nucleonics'. Below, Corfu was drawing on walls with an airily free and gracious hand. And Zook sat despondently at the foot of the staircase, muttering, 'Fungus, fungus, burn all their fungus!' hypnotically, over and over again. Kane eased past him, strode to his office but quickly stopped short as he looked at the door. Painted in glowing, intimidating purple were the letters '*W.C.*' Beneath the legend were cupid's hearts pierced by arrows, within them inscriptions. One frankly attested that '*Laurence Harvey loves Elliot Ness*'. Still another encased the legend, '*Gamal Nasser loves Golda Meir*'. And a third read,

'*Lyndon Johnson loves Ayn Rand*'. Scrawled in pencil, all over the door, were names of girls and telephone numbers as well as anatomical sketches and fragments of obscenity.

Kane breathed deeply, put a hand on the doorknob. Then suddenly whipped around as he heard a sound of ripping fabric, felt a dancing across his trousers. Confronting him was Fairbanks, poised like Scaramouche. He had slashed an 'F' into Kane's buttocks.

Fairbanks sneered at Kane contemptuously. 'There, no sniveling! You're not hurt! I just shot the gun from your hand, vile dog!'

Fromme irrupted before them, bawling, 'Get this man into surgery, dammit! He's bleeding to death! Don't you care? Judas priest, doesn't anyone *care*!'

Kane stood frozen, his eyes fixed on Fairbanks, who was dancing around him and feinting with his sword, snarling, 'Defend yourself, you churl!' Bemish dropped the hammer on Groper.

Kane suddenly turned and went into his office, slamming the door shut behind him as he moved toward his desk. He clutched at his temples, for a moment stood rigid. Then, swift as a spasm, he reached to his desk, picked up a Los Angeles telephone directory and ripped it savagely, smoothly and effortlessly into two very neatly edged halves; he flung them both against a wall.

'Great God!'

Kane whirled. Leslie Spoor stood gaping in shock. Kane said nothing, felt at his head. Spoor took a step, picked up a phone book half, eyed it numbly and then looked at Kane. 'Was that *you*, "Little Flower"?' he breathed. Then he bolted from the room, bawling, 'Manfred! Mighty Manfred!'

Kane was a man who had looked on Medusa; eyes wide and staring and yet unseeing. The jagged pulse in his cheek where once the scar had been glowed white.

CHAPTER EIGHT

'The man has a *devil*,' brooded Cutshaw, sprawled on a cot in the inmates' dorm.

'Ta! He is harmless,' responded Corfu, breathing heavily, adenoidally, over a chessboard opposite Nammack on the cot adjoining Cutshaw's. Lieutenant Nammack, a former navigator, was wearing his coonskin cap. The tip of the tail was touching the board as his head bent low in ponder.

'Don't be a child,' Cutshaw retorted. 'Kane is fox, an absolute fox. Look at his eyes. Don't you get any message?'

'Check!' said Corfu.

Cutshaw eyed him severely. 'How very like you, Master Corfu. You have eyes but will not see; ears, but will not listen.'

'Shit!' breathed Nammack.

'*What?*' demanded Cutshaw.

'He has me in check.'

Cutshaw reached out a foot and irritably swept away the chess pieces. 'Splendid,' said the astronaut. 'Your leader speaks of doom and you speak of check. Dummies, Kane has *us* in check.'

'I think him harmless,' repeated Corfu eyeing the shambles of his conquest.

'What was he doing,' insisted Cutshaw, 'in his room for ten whole days?'

'Didn't he say he was reading?' answered Nammack.

'Bah, humbug!' grumped Cutshaw. 'He harrows

me,' he fretted, 'with mighty fear and wonder.' Then his eyes stared blankly at nothing as he contemplated the deeps.

Spoor burst upon them, breathless.

'Mighty Manfred, I have news!'

'From the "Twilight Zone"?' asked Cutshaw.

Corfu and Nammack started a game.

'I speak of Kane!' declared Spoor.

'What about him?' prodded Cutshaw.

'Listen, none of him is him?'

Too weary to walk away, Cutshaw turned his back on Spoor, sighing, 'Sure, baby, sure.'

Spoor seized Cutshaw's foot, twisting the astronaut around to him. 'Gregory Peck in *Spellbound*! Remember? Remember? Supposed to be a psychiatrist, takes charge of a nut house but all the time he's crazy and not a doctor at all?'

'Hmm.'

'Same thing with Kane! Wait'll you *hear*! Wait'll you *hear*! I mean, *just* like the movie! Just *exactly* Gregory Peck!'

Spoor's dog licked Cutshaw's hand with a bubbly, liquid razor.

'I take a fork in my hand, see, a fork in my hand! On a tablecloth make ski tracks and then Kane looks down and *faints*!' Spoor leaped over to Nammack. 'Understand me? *Faints*!'

Nammack lifted his head to him, his nose but an inch from Spoor's, and as he spoke his voice grew in volume as the theme overmastered him. 'You're a very sick man, Spoor, you *know* that, baby, don't you? Now get out of my *life*, kid! Who *needs* your kind of illness! Get some *help*, professional *help*!'

'Do not mock,' Spoor uttered softly, whereupon Nammack tweaked his nose. Spoor emitted a yelp and leaped up from the cot. 'So! I come to you with goodies and you answer me with farts! That is what comes of casting Fritos among the apes! But no more! Why should I tell you about the phone book Colonel Kane ripped in half! Come, Rip Torn!' With a haughty, careless grace, Spoor tossed the neatly ripped half of the phone book onto the chessboard, and flounced imperiously away.

Cutshaw turned over, eyeing the telephone book, then called out, 'Spoor! Spoor! Hey, wait!'

'From here to eternity!' answered Spoor, turning around by the door.

'Did you *see* Kane rip it in half?'

'I have seen what I have seen! I have spake! Pox on your kidney!' fumed Spoor. Then he turned again and left them.

Corfu's eyes met Cutshaw's. 'Didn't you say he knew nothing about Rorschachs?'

'I said he *pretended* he didn't know.'

'What are you thinking?' Nammack asked Cutshaw.

'That we are all in "rats' alley where the dead men lost their bones".'

'What?'

'T. S. Eliot. I shall board the monster presently.'

'T. S. Eliot?' puzzled Nammack.

'Gregory Peck,' murmured Cutshaw.

Kane was dozing at his desk when the door slam awakened him. He jerked up his head, saw Manfred Cutshaw turning the lock, and grinning evilly. 'Spoor has told me everything, you mad, wicked boy!'

'What are you talking about?' said Kane.

Cutshaw whipped out a pen and extended it to Kane as he pressed a document flat on the desk top. 'Enough of this pretense!' he crackled. 'Here! Sign this confession, Hud! Or Greg! Or Tab! Or whoever you happen to be!'

'What in the devil do you mean?'

'I mean none of you is you!'

The crash of a hammer was heard from afar, chased by the ghosts of falling plaster. Kane's glance flicked down to the document. Then up again at Cutshaw. 'This is blank.'

'Of *course* it's blank. We aren't certain who you *are* yet. Merely sign and we'll fill it in later.'

'Cutshaw, just for the sake of humoring you—'

'*Sign* "Great Impostor"! Plead the mercy of the court. Kangaroos can be *kind*. Kangaroos are not all *bad*.'

'Tell me – who do you *think* I am?'

'I must be frank,' said the astronaut, his eyelids narrowed to slits. 'There are some who believe that Hitler is still alive. The lunatic fringe, of course.'

Again the blow of a hammer. And now the running of feet.

'And what do *you* think?' asked the Colonel.

'I'm not thinking. Not at all. I am merely taking a poll. The decision of the judges, Hud, is absolutely final.' Cutshaw again extended the pen. 'Make your "X" . . . neatness counts.'

Kane smiled at him coldly, whereupon Cutshaw retracted the pen and took a haughty step backward. 'Proud ox! Is that your answer? Very well!' He swooped to the door. 'We'll send you cigarettes and cookies every month, Colonel Bogey! Addressed, *in-*

108

cidentally, to "Occupant, Cell 108"!' He turned the lock, swung wide the door, revealing Groper beaming with triumph, Bemish's hammer held high in his hand.

'Got it!' Groper exulted.

'Marvey!' commented Cutsaw. Then he pointed to the Captain. 'Look, look, Hud! See the idiot captain! See the pretty hammer! See the idiot captain as he *swings* the pretty hammer?'

'Cutshaw!' hissed Groper.

'Kane, we are watching!' warned the astronaut grimly. Then he oozed out of sight.

'Watching what?' asked Groper.

Kane looked blank, did not answer. He merely stared at Groper fixedly. The Captain looked at the hammer, feeling sheepish and oddly uncomfortable. 'Got the hammer,' he mumbled inanely, and thought: Groper, you're okay. He tossed a salute and left the office, despising the fear that he felt in Kane's presence.

Kane looked down at the blank 'confession' form that Cutshaw had placed on his desk. He picked it up and turned it over. And blinked at the fragment of verse that he found scrawled on the back of the page:

For what to Werner von Braun is
This quintessence of dust?
'The sun, mother; give me the sun.'
Alas, poor Hamlet, he is mad.
But we'll give him Manhattan,
The Bronx and Staten Island, too,
For here the men are as made as he.
  Star light,
  Star bright,
  First nobody sees:

Not anymore.
Not tonight.
Merry Christmas, Auntie Sanger,
Merry Christmas.
Your troubles are nought.
    Twinkle
        Twinkle
            Little

BLAST!
See the mushroom, Auntie Sanger?
See the funny white mushroom?
Old Geiger counters
A few dismembered arms and
A torn and faded print of the Mona Lisa
Hurtle breathtakingly out beyond the reaches
Of Isaac Newton, becoming stars in a
Miniature universe:
The revolving, orbital ghost of all
Christmases past
And not to be.
'Mona Lisa, Mona Lisa, men have named you':
A tight-lipped
Thin-lipped
Unsmiling smile
Alone in the void:
Not one now to mock your own spinning?
Mountains and hills, come, come and fall on me!
Midnight never come.

And there is ended. Kane read it again, placing the literary allusions; they convinced him the poem was Cutshaw's. Had he intended that Kane read it? 'The sun, mother; give me the sun.' Wasn't that the line by which the boy in Ibsen's *Ghosts* disclosed to his mother that he was mad? He couldn't remember. He read the poem again. And thought it more likely that one of the fail-safe crewmen had written it. Then realized with a start that he could have written it himself.

Cutshaw returned, slamming the door. 'Now I know who you are,' he grimly announced.

'Who?'

'An unfrocked priest!' Cutshaw then took a flying leap at the sofa, sprawled on his back and clutched at his medal. 'I want you to hear my confession.'

'I'm not a priest,' said Kane.

'Hah! Also you're not an orange. Colonel No-Face, who the hell *are* you? All this suspense is a pain in the ass.'

'I am Colonel Hudson Kane.'

'You are Gregory Peck, you idiot. Don't let anyone talk you out of it. No one could ever talk *me* out of it. Not on your life. No, sir. I'd be glad to be Adolphe Menjou. Have I told you about my uncle? Played piano on a mountaintop, naked as a jaybird. Did it almost every morning, Hud, usually at sunrise.'

'Yes, go on,' said Kane.

'That's all.'

'That's all?'

'About my uncle, you mean?'

'Yes.'

'Hell, isn't that *enough*? What more do you *want*?'

'Nothing at all. I merely wondered why you mentioned it.'

'I mentioned it, you cluck, because Adolphe Menjou wouldn't *do* that. And neither would Warren Beatty. I would *love* to be Warren Beatty.'

111

'Well, I really don't see why,' said Kane.

'Of *course* you don't see why! You're Gregory *Peck*!'

'Yes, yes, I see.'

'Don't go putting me on, you patronizing snot. You're not Gregory Peck at all. You're an unfrocked priest. Incidentally, old padre, I've got some rather disquieting news for you.'

'What? What news?'

'I can prove there is a Foot. Would you like me to do it now or would you prefer to wire the Pope before I talk to United Press? Once that happens, Hud, I warn you, there won't be frocks to go around. Better put yours on now so they'll think you're sincere.'

'Let's hear the proof.'

'Put on the frock. I don't want to see you hurt.'

'I haven't *got* a frock.'

'Where the hell *is* it?' demanded Cutshaw. 'Walking around at some witches' sabbath?'

'No.'

'Hud – put on the frock.'

'The proof.'

'You crazy, stubborn kid, Hud. Don't come sniveling to me later when you can't get a job cleaning altars.' Cutshaw sat up. 'Have you ever heard of "entropy"?'

'I have.'

'Say it's a racehorse and I'll maim you!'

'It is related,' said Kane, 'to a law of thermodynamics.'

'Pretty slick there, Hud. Maybe too slick for your own damn good. Now where am I heading?' demanded Cutshaw.

'I don't know. You tell me.'

'To where the *universe* is heading! To a final, final

heat death! Know what that is? Well, I'll tell you. I am Morris the Explainer. It's a basic foos of physics, an *irreversible*, basic foos that one of these days, bye and bye, the whole damn party will be over. In about three billion years every particle of matter in the entire bloody universe will be totally disorganized. Random, totally random. And once the universe is random it'll maintain a certain temperature, a certain *constant* temperature that never, never changes. And because it never changes the particles of matter in the universe can never hope to reorganize. The universe can't build up again. Random, it'll always stay random. Forever and ever and ever. Doesn't that scare the living piss out of you, Hud? Hud, where's your frock? Got a spare? Let me have it. I shouldn't talk like this in front of me. I swear, it gives me the willies.'

As Cutshaw spoke, he stared at the ground, like a man who is talking to himself.

'Please continue,' said Colonel Kane.

'Do you accept my foos of physics?'

'Theories keep changing every year,' said Kane. 'But this one seems immutable. At least, the physicists seem to think so.'

'Does that mean "yes", you devious asp?'

'Yes.'

'You accept my basic foos?'

'Yes, I accept it.'

Cutshaw scowled, looking up. 'Don't say "it", you swine, say *"foos"*. Say, "I accept your basic foos." '

Kane gripped a pencil under the desk and broke it in half. Then looked at his hands. 'I accept your basic foos.'

'Marvey keen! Now follow, Youngblood, follow.

113

Follow very, very carefully.' Cutshaw's speech became slow and measured. 'It's a matter of *time* before it happens, before we reach that final heat death. And when we reach that final heat death, life can never reappear. If that seems clear, Hud, paw the ground twice.'

'Yes, that's clear.'

'Your lightning insights purely astound me. Now, let's take a simple disjunction. Either matter – matter or energy – is eternal and always existed, or it *didn't* always exist and had a definite beginning in time. So let's eliminate one or the other. Let's say that matter always existed. And bear in mind that the coming heat death, Hud, is purely a matter of time. Did I say three billion years? Let's say a *billion* billion years. I don't care *what* the time required is, Hud. Whatever it is, it's limited. But if matter always existed, dunce, you and I aren't here.'

'What?'

'Hud, we don't *exist*! Heat death has already come and gone!'

'I don't follow.'

'You'd rather confess. Give me the frock and I'll let you confess. Let no one write "*Obdurate*" on my tombstone. Call me flexible, Hud, and confess.'

'Captain—'

'Warren, then. Call me Warren.'

'I've missed a connection,' said Kane, 'in the argument.'

'You've been missing connections the whole of your life! Foot! You are dumber than a prize Dauphin. Look – if matter has always existed and if heat death is a matter of time like, let's say, a billion billion years, then, Hud, it's got to have *already happened*! A billion

billion years have come and gone a trillion times, *mon cher*, an *infinite* number of times! Ahead of us and behind us, is an infinite number of years in the case of matter always existing! So heat death has come and gone! And once it comes, there can never be life! Never again! Not for eternity! So how come we're talking, eh, how come? Though notice that *I* am talking *sensibly* while you just sit there *drooling*. Nevertheless, we are here. Why is that?'

Interest quickened in Kane's eyes. 'Either matter is not eternal, I'd say, or the entropy theory is wrong.'

'*What*? You reject my basic foos, Hud? My basic foos of *physics*?'

'No,' said Kane. 'No, I do not.'

'Then there can be only one alternative, Greg: matter *hasn't* always existed. And that means once there was purely *nothing*, Hud, nothing at all in existence. So how come there's something *now*? The answer is obvious to even the lowliest, the meanest of intelligences, and that, of course, means you. The answer is something *other* than matter had to make matter begin to be. That something other I call Foot. How does that grab you?'

'It's rather compelling.'

'There's only one thing wrong,' said Cutshaw.

'What?'

'I don't believe it for a minute. What do you take me for, a lunatic?' The astronaut sprang from the sofa, charging the desk with head-bent belligerence. 'I copied that proof from a privy wall at a Maryknoll Mission in Beverly Hills!'

'It doesn't convince you?'

'Intellectually, yes. But emotionally, *no*!'

Kane said, 'I thought you'd made it up.'

'Hud, I am *sick* of your snotty insults. Sick of your whole performance, in fact! Enough of this shabby charade! Burn your frock! Buy a gown! You are Mary Baker Eddy!'

Kane said, 'I thought I was Gregory Peck.'

'Why, you incredible megalomaniac! How come you're loose while your betters are chained!'

'Please sit down,' motioned Kane.

'No, I won't.'

'Cutshaw, why not?'

'There is quicksand all around me. Think I'm a child? Think I'm a Kane? Think that I'd fall for *that* dumb trick? Next you'll say, "Look at the submarine!" and then you'll squirt me with a water gun!' The astronaut leaped onto the desk, sitting with folded arms and legs, confronting Kane like a Delphic leprechaun. 'Lieutenant Zook thinks you're P. T. Barnum,' he said. 'I thought him to be in error at first and declared him excommunicate, but perhaps I overextended. I see on your brow the Mark of the Beast.'

'What?' Kane subtly stiffened.

'Have you ever killed a lamb?'

'No.'

'Barnum slaughtered a thousand. He set up a cage at one of his sideshows, put in a lion and a lamb. Side by side. Lion and lamb. And there was never any trouble. Hud, the public just went lollypops. "Look, a lion and a lamb," they said, "and they never even argue! Hell, they never even *discuss*!" It was spookier than plastic figs. But what the public didn't know was that it was never the same lamb. It was always the same lion, though, one with regular eating habits, always at intermission. Ate a lamb every day for almost three hundred days. Then they shot him for asking for mint sauce. As for myself, I would have shot Barnum.'

'I have never killed a lamb,' said Kane, his tongue thick in his mouth.

'Why should *anyone* kill a lamb? It isn't the killing, it's the suffering. Why should *any* animal suffer?'

Kane said softly, 'Why should *man*?'

'None of that, you frockless seducer. Human suffering admits of answers. "Pie in the sky" and other inanities of the same stupid kidney. But animals *get* no pie in the sky. Let's talk about *them* and avoid the piosities, Hud. Why should animals suffer?'

Kane said simply, 'Man must eat.'

'Let 'em eat *cake*!' roared Cutshaw abruptly. 'Anyway, who ever ate a vulture? Why do *vultures* have to suffer!'

'Pain is a necessary evil. Not evil at all, in fact, but a warning device that acts for the good of the body.'

'That is bullcrap, pure and simple. That has nothing to do with vultures. Hell, a man can thrive on mother's milk, on wheat germ, or *grass*! Why eat meat? Why does he have to? For cholesterol and a heart attack? Why have animals at *all* if they've got to gore each others' stomachs' just to *live*, Colonel Fiasco! Is there an afterlife for animals? A balance for the pain? Would you say that pain makes vultures "noble"? Gives them "character"? Crap like that? If there is a Foot and he made panthers, then he surely must have *bunions*! I can't *believe* in such a Foot!'

'How do you know,' Kane reasoned quietly, 'that an animal's experience of pain is anything like what it

117

is for man? Isn't pain more intense with cognition? With memory of what it is like?'

Cutshaw glared for a moment in silence. Then reached out his hand and cuffed Kane's ear. 'After an answer so zestfully fatuous, I feel I must terminate this discussion. You are a donkey without peer and totally useless, to me, useless.'

Cutshaw nimbly leaped from the desk, whipped a document from his pocket and spread it flat in front of Kane. 'Kindly sign this confession so we can all get a little peace. Please do not sign it "Calvin Coolidge" or any such subtle attempt at forgery. Fun is fun but we've had enough. Do you drink Coke?'

'No, I don't.'

'Colonel Ryan was a Mormon. *He* drank Coke and thought he sinned heinously.'

'What is the point?' asked Colonel Kane.

'How should *I* know?' yipped the astronaut. 'I never pretended that I know *every*thing! Now sign. A simple "A" will do. "A" for Attila the Hun.'

Kane looked at Cutshaw intently. 'Why do you call me "Attila the Hun"?'

'Why do you call me Manfred Cutshaw? Everyone *knows* I'm Warren Beatty. Come, now, sign, I'm through protecting you.'

'Let's talk,' said Kane.

'Indeed. I propose that we talk about my uncle. Now he's a general in the Air Force. Sits twenty-four hours in a Pentagon basement with his fingers twitching near buttons and a bright-red meltproof phone. Still naked as a jaybird, Hud, but hell, he gets no visitors, so I figure, what's the harm. Sign the confession.'

118

'Let's talk about God.'

'Not with you. All your knowledge is pure Quinsana. Now make your "A"; I'm getting restless.'

Kane glanced at the paper, then up at Cutshaw. 'What do you know?' he asked him cryptically.

'That I can walk like a fly.' Cutshaw abruptly flew at a wall, making several earnest attempts at running straight up the side of it while singing an aria from *Carmen*. After his fifth abortive attempt, he cast an accusing look at Kane. 'There's something wrong with this wall,' he glared, then crouched, like Richard the Third, out of the office with a glide. 'We are watching!' he warned from the doorway, and melted away like morning mist.

Kane turned over the blank confession form, stared at a penciled sketch depicting two peering eyes. And felt the first faint pulsations of an imminent migraine headache.

Cutshaw leaned out of a dormitory window, deep in brood. Zook stood beside him, training binoculars on the school next door, Clydene Sloop, he had long since discovered, was a shameless exhibitionist who did most of her studying naked with her window blinds up full. No doubt it improved her concentration, thought Zook, who was rarely inclined to be cynical. He was purely and simply inclined, and accepted whatever heaven sent without question. However, at the moment Clydene was not in, and all he could find was Mary Jo Mawr, pensively brooding out her window like dark-eyed Bess, the innkeeper's daughter.

'That phone-book trick,' muttered Cutshaw. 'Wish I'd seen it for myself.'

'Starting to doubt?'

'Let's shake him up. Really press him. Maybe – maybe he'll lose his grip. Suppose one of us grabbed him by surprise when we've really got him going?'

'Leave him alone,' said Zook.

The astronaut softly uttered, 'I can't.' Then he turned to Zook with fresh attack. 'Come on, you start it. Get on him right now.'

'*Now?*'

'Now!'

Zook was torn. Clydene had appeared. But her slink was no match for Cutshaw's command. Zook put away the binoculars and moved toward the dormitory door, muttering of fardels and Cutshaw's contumely.

Kane was in the hall. Captain Groper had approached him with deference, suggesting the men had 'too much freedom' and needed a far 'firmer hand.' Kane cited Ryan's experience, his head aching unbearably, and advised the captain not to 'meddle.' Groper was leaving as Zook approached.

'Herod Agrippa, where is my belt! Where is my Buck Rogers *flying* belt!'

'It's coming,' lied Kane; 'it's coming; it's coming.'

'Why is it *gone*?' Zook suddenly shrieked. Then leaned in his head conspiratorially, speaking in almost a whisper. 'The brain named Cutshaw,' he advised the Colonel, 'says you're not a brain at all.'

'Oh?'

'Yes. That's what he said. He said that your name is Sybilline Books. On the level, now, tell me – is it true?'

'No, it isn't.'

'Damnit, who can I *believe*!' bawled Zook. Then again he lowered his voice. 'Listen, he offered me a deal,' he rasped. 'He said if I gave him the map coordinates of the factory on my planet that manufactures all those Beatle wigs, he'd get me back the belt. But I was loyal. Understand? I told him *no*, that you'd feel *hurt*. No, no, no, no, I cannot lie; I cannot lie to you, kindly brain, kindly *compassionate* giant brain. Yes, I'll admit that at first I was *weak*. Yes! At first, I'll admit, I said "Deal!" But as soon as I said, "Deal!" he added on another condition. Know what he wanted? That *filth*? He wanted "secret information on who Orphan Annie sleeps with!" Yes! Orphan Annie! How did he *know* about Orphan Annie? Did you pick my brain and *tell* him?'

'I did not,' said Kane very softly.

'*Who can I trust!*' shrieked Dorian Zook. Then he eyed Kane levelly, spoke in a flat expressionless voice. 'Orphan Annie does not sleep. She's a cartoon, just a cartoon. I give you that information gratis as a token of my goodwill.'

'Very good of you.'

'Nothing. Hell, I'd do it for an Earthman. Now *reciprocate*, you bastard, or I'll make the deal with Cutshaw!' The pilot's voice grew loud and shrill. 'I might find a way to *kill* you; give you ultimate migraine *headache*! Where's the *belt*!'

'It's on order.'

'Order from where? Sears and Roebuck? Make a movement, idiot brain, and pull your tentacles out of your fanny! We're on *Venus*, the planet *Venus*! What do you take me for, a stoop? Why do you think my government picked me? Because I see real good in *space*? I've had all the crap and hocus-pocus I can take! Understand? Produce the belt in twenty-four hours or you're in horribly deep trouble! Now go and wrap yourself in fronds or whatever you do when you have to sleep! I am sealing off my mind!'

Zook departed, leaving Kane drained, his head now throbbing even more painfully. Kane took dinner in his office. Floating atop his alphabet soup, glued together farinaceously were the letters *c-o-n-f-e-s-s*. He could not finish the soup.

Kane went to his room and found on a wall, smeared in mustard, the message: *'Hud! We Can Be Lenient!'* Still another was on a mirror: *'There Is Foot Powder in Heaven for Those Who Repent!'* Kane went to his bathroom, wet a towel, quickly wiped away the messages. Then he stripped to his shorts, slid into bed and tried to make his mind a blank. His lips moved incessantly, forming words without utterances. He slipped to the edge of dreams. Fragments . . . the Mona Lisa . . . Bemish's hammer circled by atoms . . . Kane sat upright with a start. He looked at his hands; they were trembling. His body was soaked with sweat. Then he heard rapping at the door.

Kane whipped aside his blanket, climbed out of bed and went to the door. He opened it, saw Fell. And imagined he saw, peripherally, the long trailing folds of a woman's black gown disappearing around a corner.

Kane abruptly remembered Fell. The medic was dressed in immaculate uniform, a dossier in his hands. He was staring at Kane in his shorts. 'I see Fromme has decided to promote himself,' he said, his words somewhat slurred.

'Where have you been?' asked Kane. He hadn't seen the doctor in days.

'Oh, here and there; hither and yon.' Fell was un-equivocally weaving, striving desperately for aplomb.

122

'Did you see a woman a moment ago? Someone wearing a black gown?'

'No,' said Fell, 'but I have seen mermaids. A common delusion of lonely men.' Then he flourished the dossier. 'Here's the file on an incoming kook. I think he's due to arrive tonight.'

'What is the time?' asked Kane.

'Nine-ish.'

'Come in.'

Fell followed him into the room. Kane snatched cigarettes from a nightstand, quickly lit one and inhaled; inhaled very deeply. His back was to Fell as he moved to a window. Abruptly he froze as he saw a message on the slat of the Venetian blind: *'Who the Hell Are You, Colonel Spook!'* Kane flipped the blinds, only to find, on the other side, another message: *'Hud, Be Reasonable! Manfred Cutshaw Saves and Satisfies!'* Kane yanked the blinds upward as Fell moved in behind him, muttering, 'One if by land and two if by sea. Baby, don't mix them up; there was *hell* to pay the last time.' Kane turned and faced him.

Fell looked Kane up and down. 'For a guy who's spent most of his life with his nose in a book, you're a pretty rugged brute,' he said. 'Where did you get those scars?'

Kane looked blank. 'What scars?'

'The ones on your leg. They're rather deep.'

Kane dredged up a smile; it was a greeting card edged in black. 'Rose thorns,' he uttered softly.

For a moment Fell made no answer. Then, 'If a woman ever asks you, tell her you got 'em in a knife fight. Grabs 'em every time.'

'I'll remember that,' said Kane. 'What's in the file?'

Fell traced some lines with a finger, then stopped, cleared his throat of phlegm, and read: '. . . Minutes before reaching the fail-safe point, the co-pilot Captain Hooker, reported hydraulic malfunction, and at this precise moment subject officer reportedly stood up, ripped off his goggles, and then his helmet, and announced in a very clear voice: "This is a case for Superman!" Subject officer then embarked upon a spirited but abortive attempt to completely strip away his flight suit, causing temporary loss of control of the aircraft . . .' Fell looked up at Kane. 'Want to hear any more?'

'That's quite enough.'

'I guess. Yeah, I guess.' Fell closed the dossier. 'How's it coming?'

'All right. Yes. All right.'

Fell eyed him for a moment and seemed about to speak, but then apparently decided against it. 'Goodnight,' he said. And left.

Outside in the hall, Kane heard him trip and fall; and then his voice, slurred and muttery: 'Confounded shoes! Why don't they make them so people don't keep falling all over them!' Then footsteps, erratic, fading.

Kane leaned against the door, when from below came a clapping of hands, the voices of inmates all singing together. The song they were singing was, 'I'm Confessin'.' Kane's head began to pound. The singing grew louder, the clapping more frenzied. Kane cupped his hands against his ears, then opened the door and went outside.

Captain Groper was at the balustrade, staring down at the dormitory door. Kane came beside him. Groper looked at him. 'Keeping my distance like you said, sir.' He smirked and walked away.

Kane hustled down the stairs, tried the dormitory door and found it locked. He knocked. The singing stopped. After a moment the door swung wide and he stook confronting Zook. 'If you came without the *belt*, sweetheart, turn around and go back!'

Kane eased past him. The inmates all sat on their cots, hunched over cards. Manfred Cutshaw stood by the fireplace, cranking a round wire basket, wooden balls clicking within it. Cutshaw extracted one of the balls and called out: 'O-sixty-seven.'

'*Bingo!*' yelped Fairbanks, racing to Cutshaw with his card. Some of the other men said 'Shit!' while the remainder muttered and mumbled. Cutshaw eyed them sternly.

'Now, now, children, it's only a game,' he said, serene as a nun at matins. Then suddenly he looked to Kane, threw up his hands in wild surprise. 'Wait! He's come!' he cried. 'He's come! Children, it's Hud! He's seen the light!' Shoving Fairbanks aside, Cutshaw rushed toward Kane, calling, 'Pen and paper, quickly! We'll take his confession while repentance still rages in his bowels!' En route, he leaned over Spoor, instructing, 'Check Fairbanks' card! He cheats!' Spoor moved forward.

Kane waited, arms akimbo, by the dormitory door, until Cutshaw was upon him, pen and paper in hand. 'Heaven be praised!' wailed the astronaut. 'Sign and all is forgiven!'

'No more singing. I want you all quiet. No more of these games,' instructed Kane.

'But Mystery Colonel, we *have* to sing! We sing

125

when a man gets "Bingo"! It's the prize! It's all we've *got*!' Cutshaw turned and bawled at the inmates, 'Children, let's give Fairbanks his song: "Nearer My Foot to Thee," number eighty-three on your cards.' Then he whirled back at Kane as the men began to sing. 'Now, then, *sign*!' he demanded harshly.

Both men turned at the crash of the hammer. Bemish was soberly demolishing a wall as Corfu kept a pace ahead of him, painting bull's-eyes for him to aim at, urging. 'Punch, lunatic, punch! Punch! Punch! Make a Swiss cheese!'

Spoor's dog began to howl and bark as Fairbanks menaced his master with his sword, shouting, 'How *dare* you accuse me of cheating! Churlish knave! Beg forgiveness or I will slit you! Yes, I will slit you high and wide!'

Spoor cried, 'Sic 'im, Julius, sic 'im! He's Brutus! He's Brutus!'

Rip Torn leaped at Fairbanks, dripping jaws clamping his ankle. 'Call off your dragon!' roared Fairbanks. 'Call him off! Call him off!'

Spoor looked to Zook, pointing imperiously at Fairbanks. 'Guard,' he bawled, '*seize* him!'

The dog was snarling, Bemish was pounding and the inmates had segued from 'I'm Confessin'' into 'Fly Me to the Moon.' Kane ran a hand across his eyes, vaguely aware that it was trembling, vaguely aware that his back was arched.

Nammack moved behind him, preparing as planned, to seize him. Neither Nammack nor Colonel Kane saw the newcomer at the door. He was a tall, bespectacled captain toting a duffel bag over his shoulder. He dropped the bag, removed his glasses, smoothly folded

126

and tucked them away. Before Nammack could move he'd stepped in to Kane, murmuring, 'This is a case for Superman!'

Kane's first awareness of the Captain was of an arm hooked around his neck. And without thinking, without knowing, Kane hurled the Captain over his shoulder, sent him flying twenty feet forward, sent him crashing against a cot, the cot slamming back into still another. The Captain slumped, semi-conscious, his head propped up against a mattress. Corfu stopped painting, Bemish stopped pounding, Fairbanks stopped feinting with his sword. And abruptly the inmates stopped singing. They slowly stood up, awed and transfixed as they gaped at the new arrival. Then they gradually turned to Kane. He was rigid, staring at the Captain.

Fairbanks lowered his sword, breathing. 'Great day in the morning! I believe we have had an event!'

Everyone froze in tableau. In the pulsing, incredulous silence, the new arrival, a Captain Alterman, shook the thunder from his head, mumbling, 'Kryptonite, yes, it was Kryptonite. Helpless against it; helpless. Never fear, boys and girls, I always come back. I always——' He stopped, seeing Kane. A look of doubt, then of wonder, then of blazing recognition leaped to his face. 'Holy Toledo!' gasped Captain Alterman. 'No wonder! *"Killer" Kane!*'

CHAPTER NINE

At age nineteen he'd flown a bomber, plastering cities in World War II. Before that he'd been an orphan, raised by gentle Franciscan brothers in San Mateo, California. The rule of charity still clung to his neck like a weeping white monkey as he opened bomb-bay doors. Once he had wanted to be a priest. In a dream he'd seen Christ beckoning warmly, telling him, 'Come, follow Me.' The dream exploded with Pearl Harbor.

In '44 the monkey wailed louder when he bailed out over Germany. Alone and unassisted, he made it back to Allied lines. En route, he slaughtered some of the enemy: four with his pistol, six with his knife, and twelve with his large and powerful hands. Somewhere deep, deep in his brain, something else had seemed to die. He heard the sighing, faint and sad, as whatever it was gave up its spirit.

At the end of the war, he stayed in the Air Corps, for there were rumors of Armageddon and he felt the goard of purpose. The monkey ceased to chatter. Then Korea shattered the peace, and the Air Force reassessed his record. They ordered him to 'Survival School' to learn the higher techniques of what seemed his natural bent and talent. Trained, he would drop behind enemy lines, perform some vital clandestine mission, then return, usually unaided, to United Nations lines.

He killed another thirty-three: this time with a wire, deftly beheading his victims before they could utter a warning gasp.

With spluttering peace he became an instructor; taught others to maim, bloody and kill. And taught supremely well. Wherever the balance of power was threatened, wherever 'brushfire' wars erupted, he was there to teach – and lead. He won the rank of full colonel and the nickname 'Killer' Kane. And on his soul, carved indelibly, were eighty-one notches. He did not know their names.

In the spring of '65 he was ordered to Vietman. At first he trained helicopter pilots in the tactics of survival. But when Vietcong guerrillas grew bolder, harassing Marines at Danang, he was put in command of special patrols that nightly seeped beyond the listening posts, counterspooking the infiltrators; discouraging penetration. It was on one of these patrols that a Marine Corps sergeant discovered him standing by a tree in the dusk with vacant eyes.

'Colonel Kane, it's almost light,' whispered the sergeant at the rendezvous; then noticed the blood streaking the greasepaint on Kane's face and hands; followed his stare to the jungle floor, and saw the bleeding, headless body. Vietcong. Very young. Perhaps no more than fifteen.

'He spoke to me,' Kane said dully.

The sergeant looked around for the head. Then gasped with horror as he saw it rolling down an incline from the tree trunk, overcoming the pressure of weeds. It thudded gently against Kane's foot.

'He spoke to me,' Kane repeated. Then he lifted his eyes to the sergeant's. 'After I killed him,' he said.

The sergeant looked suddenly alarmed. 'Jesus, Colonel, let's get back!'

'He said I loved him,' Kane said softly.

'Christ, *forget* about it, Colonel!' The sergeant took him by the arm, squeezing deep with steely fingers. Then he rasped, 'Colonel, *forget* it!' and savagely kicked away the head, fighting an instant impulse to vomit. Suddenly Kane ripped free from his grip. His eyes seemed to clear.

'Come on, let's go,' he ordered the sergeant in a tone that was brisk and commanding. The sergeant returned with him to base. Said nothing. And pondered.

In days to come Kane was to wonder why the sergeant, whenever he saw him, would eye him oddly, almost in puzzlement: the look of a man who has asked a question, then suddenly hoped he would get no answer. Kane had completely forgotten the incident. But something within him had remembered. He made sure that the sergeant never again accompanied him on patrol. He could think of no special reason, except that it somehow seemed more efficient. Beneath this glaze of motivation, he was careful never to probe.

Some two weeks after the incident Kane was standing by a window of his adjutant's sandbagged shack, staring out at torrential rains that had not ceased for the last four days. The adjutant, Lieutenant Bidwill, was hunched over a TWX machine that noisily spewed out messages a chattering eighth of an inch per thrust. It mingled in ominous syncopation with the pounding of the rain. Kane suddenly started; then relaxed. He'd heard a voice, he thought, from the jungle: a single cry that sounded like 'Kane!' Then he'd seen the bird taking off from the treetops and he remembered the screech of its species.

An orderly, carrying food on a tray, came in through the open door. 'Ready for lunch now, Colonel Kane?'

Kane had heard the orderly's footsteps, but continued to stare out the window. He remembered steaming mugs of cocoa frosty mornings, yes, and evenings, at the orphanage long ago. He could never get enough of it. There'd been a brother – Brother Charles – who would tousle his hair and call him 'Cocoa-top'. 'You're turning to chocolate,' he'd say; then sometimes look sad and walk away. There was no cocoa now in the rations. 'Never enter this office,' Kane said edgily, 'without knocking, Private Miller. Try it again; this time with knuckles.'

'Yes, *sir!*'

Kane heard the orderly retreating; felt an unaccountable trembling in his fingers; a twitching in his bones. These were his constant companions ever since coming to Vietnam. Nor could he sleep; at best, an hour or two each night; and the strings of sleep were plucked by dreams, chilling nightmares always forgotten. He tried to remember them but couldn't. There were times when he was dreaming when he would tell himself in the dream that surely this time he would remember. He never did. Not once. The morning's only legacy was sweat and the buzz of mosquitoes. Only that. No more. Yet the dreams, he knew, never left him; still ran darkly through his subconscious like an underground channel for sewage; eyes of rats, sleek and slimy, gleaming bright, gleaming assurance, fixed on some easy prey within him. Behind him he sensed vague tracks; was nagged by a prescience of imminent disaster.

'If it were done when it were done,' murmured Kane.

'Sir?' queried Bidwill.

'Macbeth,' said Kane. 'You should read more, Lieutenant; makes the jungle almost bearable.'

Kane heard the orderly's knock. Then footsteps halting beside him. 'Ready for lunch now, Colonel?'

The sentence was never completed. Kane chopped out irritably with his hand, sending the tray and all of its contents shattering noisily to the floor. 'Get that fungus out of my sight!' he rasped, never turning his gaze from the window.

Private Miller raced out of the room. Lieutenant Bidwill looked up at Kane. His face was a mask without expression, and yet in his eyes there flickered a sadness, a questioning wonder flecked with fear. Then once more he looked to the TWX machine as it clicked its teeth without pause.

'Can't you turn that damn thing off!' snapped Kane.

'Special orders coming in, sir.' Abruptly the machine fell silent. Bidwill grunted; then he snorted; then he ripped away the message. When he looked up, the Colonel was gone; rain splattered in through an open door. He raced to the doorway, saw the Colonel walking slowly toward the jungle; coatless, hatless, instantly drenched in the violent downpour. The Lieutenant shook his head. Again there was sadness in his eyes. And gentle concern in his summoning voice: 'Colonel! Colonel Kane, sir!'

Kane stopped dead, turned and faced him, eyes on

his hands that were cupped before him, like a child catching the rain.

The Lieutenant flourished the TWX. 'Colonel Kane! Please come in, sir!'

Kane walked slowly back to the shack, stood silently staring at Bidwill as trickles of water plopped down from the cuffs of his trousers and sleeves, puddling the floor.

Bidwill held out the TWX. 'Sir, I thought this might give you a laugh.'

'What is it?'

'Orders reassigning you to Los Angeles, California.'

Kane stared numbly at the Lieutenant. 'Where?'

'Stateside, sir! Los Angeles! But it's an obvious mistake.'

Kane took the TWX and started to read it as the Lieutenant rattled on, straining for lightness in his voice. 'Puts you in charge of some kind of asylum. Man, what a rock!' He fingered a place on the message. 'Got you confused with someone else. See? Calls you a psychologist. Also wrong middle initial.'

The Lieutenant moved to a desk, picked up a pipe and began to fill it. 'Sir, I only hope the Russians are as fouled up as we are. If computers cut their assignments, then I'm damned sure that they are.' He briefly laughed through his nose. 'I know some clerks as dumb as computers, but they don't cost millions of dollars and some are a hell of a lot more charming. Take that typist in—'

He turned and Kane was gone. He was walking in the rain. On the floor was the crumpled TWX. Bidwill soberly walked to the door, grimaced as raindrops splattered his face. The orderly, back to clean up, walked up beside him, started out at Kane. 'What is it with him?' he asked the Lieutenant.

'I just told him a funny joke.'

Night fell suddenly. The Lieutenant paced in his quarters, chain-smoking nervously. Kane had been gone for hours. What should he do? Send out a patrol? He would like to avoid it if he could; avoid the necessity of explaining that 'Colonel Kane took a walk in the rain without a hat, without a coat, but I thought it in keeping with his recent behavior, which has generally seemed unglued.' He was protective about the Colonel. Everyone else regarded Kane with a mixture of awe, dislike and fear, but for Bidwill he'd lowered the veil: treated him gently; sometimes with fondness; allowed him to glimpse, from time to time, a sensitive boy who was hopelessly trapped inside a massive suit of armor. Bidwill responded with stubborn loyalty. This, in turn, had prompted compassion when Kane's behavior turned erratic. The Lieutenant suspected what was happening. Yet he feared to give it a name.

Bidwill crushed out a cigarette, picked up his pipe and chewed on the stem. Then he saw Kane in the open doorway. Drenched, sopping wet, he was faintly smiling at his adjutant. 'Lieutenant,' he said, 'Lieutenant – if we could scrub away the blood, do you think we could find where we've hidden our souls?' Before the Lieutenant could answer, he'd walked away and down the hall. Bidwill heard, with great relief, the muted closing of his door.

The following morning Kane told Bidwill that he was leaving, complying with orders. The Lieutenant said nothing about the 'mistake'. But when he gave the TWX to mimeo for the cutting of ample copies, he made two slight and deft alterations. Instead of 'Hudson L. Kane,' it now read 'Hudson O. Kane'; and it no longer specified 'psychologist'. Kane never mentioned whether or not he had noticed it. But just before boarding the Air Force helicopter that was to take him to the capital, he stared at Bidwill intently, shook his hand and said simply, 'Thank you.'

The Lieutenant wished him good luck.

The Cure

CHAPTER TEN

When the message arrived from Lastrade, General Syntax was answering questions on a television program called 'Meet the L. A. Press.' Ordinarily 'live', this particular session was being taped because the General had insisted that 'in the interest of national security, certain editing might be needed.' Studio heads had grumbled, but after the first fifteen minutes of taping, both the producer and the director breathed a prayer of silent thanksgiving for the General's demand, for by then it was clear to both of them that editing *would* be required to achieve the basic, minimal requisite of simple declarative sentences in any of the General's answers. Out of ninety minutes of tape, roughly sixty minutes of 'uhs', 'wells', and both the definite and indefinite articles wound up in a wire basket on the cutting-room floor, where that evening a startled scrub-woman swore that when she looked at it, she'd heard 'someone clearing his throat at the bottom of the basket.' No one dared to say she'd imagined it.

When Syntax reached his office, General Lastrade was awaiting him, impatiently hurling darts at a wall map of the world. 'About time,' gruffed Lastrade, his cigar twitching impatiently at the corner of his mouth. 'What did you say,' he asked, 'on that show?'

Syntax said, 'Nothing!', and looked proud.

'Good! Good!' throated Lastrade, winging a dart into Trucial Oman and hoping that Syntax was telling the truth. He remembered how once, on a network radio show, Syntax referred to De Gaulle as a 'frog.' Like a peaceful old dog asleep in the sun, Syntax was likely, at any moment, to suddenly waken and bite someone's leg.

'Senator Hesburgh's in Los Angeles on vacation,' Lastrade explained. 'Now what about Cutshaw? How's he coming? What about all those other creeps? What do you hear from the "Little Flower"?'

'I said nothing,' Syntax said dully. He was still thinking about the panel show. So far as he could remember, he had answered most of the questions in the words of Sir Roger de Coverley: 'There's much to be said on both sides.' But then, anything was possible, he thought, in a rapid and heated exchange. He awoke to find General Lastrade gently pricking his ear with the point of a dart, snarling, '*Back,* Sheba, *back!*'

Lastrade went through it again, concluding. 'The senator might get cozy, sneak an inspection out at the farm. I promised to take him there myself, but then that filibustering bastard's likely to wing out on his own. I've got a tail on him, just in case; couple of boys from OSI. Now what's the score? Any progress? When's the last time you were there?'

'Uh – when I dropped off Colonel Kane.'

'When you dropped off Colonel Kane.'

'Yes.'

Lastrade, in a sermon of fire, then instructed General Syntax on the prudence and practical merit of hieing his person out to the mansion. 'Or would you rather,' bawled Lastrade, 'that I order an air strike on your billet!' Syntax saw no point in the latter.

Why did I do it? wondered Kane.

He sat at his desk, his head in his hands. The mansion was quiet. Nothing stirred. The silence was heavy, thick, like waiting, ever since Kane, the night before, had fled from the dorm and from Captain Alterman; from his startled recognition based on a course in survival tactics taken from Kane years ago in Korea. He'd run to his room and locked the door. But no one approached him, no one had knocked. Same thing this morning. No one. Nothing.

'Why did I do it?' Kane murmured aloud. What did I mean that night in the rain? What did I mean when I said that to Bidwill – scrubbing the blood? finding our souls? At the time, he remembered, he'd known; had felt a wave of exhilaration. And yet now it was like his dreams: he was awake and could not remember. Something. What? Defiance? Partly. Yes, partly; partly that. And something to do with killing. Blood. No more killing. And yet more, much more. Probing tentacles of memory dipped frantically into the wood, into that rainy jungle night when he'd heard that urgent inner voice, irresistible in its command, insist he accept the mistaken assignment. What had it said? What was its warning? Yes! *Warning*! he realized abruptly. The voice gave a warning! What was the warning? Kane groped for the words, then gave up the search, fell back into brooding, hopeless lethargy. Impersonating a psychologist. It seemed now the impetuous act of a madman. He'd known all along they would find him out; that sooner or later the tape would unsnarl. Meantime, what was it he'd hoped to accomplish?

Kane rested his head on top of the desk, straining to

remember; and slept for ten minutes; deeply; heavily. Kane dreamed. It was disjointed, wildly jumbled. And in places contradictory. First, he was in Korea, some-place far beyond the Parallel, kneeling over a body, a dripping wire still in his hand. The enemy (enemy?) was in the habit of a Franciscan. He turned the body over. And recognized the face. It was kindly Brother Charles. Sweet Brother Charles. And at the very same time it was Cutshaw. He was dead but still alive. And in Kane's mind he was also Father Zossima in *The Brothers Karamazov*. 'Hell,' said Zossima-Cutshaw-Charles, 'is the inability to love.' Kane plucked out a knife and stabbed at the heart, and said, 'I'm sorry, I have to do it.' Then he kissed his victim's cheek and said, 'I'm crazy! Yes, I'm crazy! I'm St. Caribou of the Cross!' Then Kane was walking in the jungle, stolidly walking in the rain. A giant white mouse stepped out in front of him; out from behind the trunk of a tree. 'You're out of your mind,' it said. 'Vivisect me!' And abruptly the wood became Molokai, and Colonel Kane was Father Damien who had come to cure the lepers. No – come to cure *himself*. Was he a leper? Some-thing like that. Suddenly Cutshaw appeared before him, but the astronaut's face was blank and eroded. 'I know who you are,' he said with cunning. And abruptly became a foot. Then Kane was sitting in a straw-thatched hut on Molokai, but he was also at the orphanage and Brother Charles was lecturing, standing at a blackboard, saying: 'Don't drop bombs, you bastards!' Then Brother Charles began to bleed – from the palms – from the feet. Out of his side there sprouted a lily. Kane jumped up by his desk and shouted, 'Brother, you said to respect authority!' And then the roof fell in upon them as bombs struck Molokai. 'Get out of here!' gasped the Franciscans. 'Get out of here! Get out! There's still time! Get the hell out!' 'I'm staying with *you*!' cried Kane in the dream. The Franciscan's head came loose from his body and Kane picked it up and fervently kissed it. 'Staying with you! Staying with you!' Then he hurled it away in revulsion. The head said, 'Feed my sheep.'

Kane awakened with an inchoate shout. Then observed that his phone was ringing. It was Syntax, calling to advise that he was on his way to see him. Kane hung up with a sense of doom. For now he remembered why he had come. Wasn't it simply to balance the scales? No, not balance; that was impossible. But some leavening act of grace; saving Cutshaw and the inmates – that much had certainly been within reach. Gone with discovery; now; gone. Syntax undoubtedly had been told.

Kane waited for the General. And groped for details of his dream. Once again he was nagged by doubts, by the question of why he had really come. Saving the men – was that all of the answer? He'd thought he could do it. But how was that possible? How could he dare where the experts had failed. Feverish study? Instinct? Intelligence? Or was it that vague and puzzling feeling that he was somehow inside their world; that where others peered in, he looked out and around?

Syntax arrived an hour later, asked that the men be formed for inspection. He made no other significant comment.

Kane stood beside him watching formation minutes later in the courtyard. Syntax scruted him, after a time, his face a portrait in colors of shock. 'I can't . . . *believe* it! Colonel Kane, this is – well – well, I'm shaken to my *roots*! To my very – you know – foun*dation*! This is absolutely (a very long pause) *splendid*!' finished the General.

Colonel Kane shared his bewilderment. First the keeping of his secret, then the behavior of the inmates set him to feverish, dizzying ponder. The inmates' uniforms were immaculate, starched and without wrinkle. Their line was neat and trim as an honor guard's, their posture stiff and proud. And as Groper called the roll, each man answered crisply, '*Here*, sir!'

'Marvelous!' burbled Syntax. 'It's simply – well – I mean – incredible change of – uh – the way they all—' Birdlike, he turned to Kane, and said, 'You follow me?'

'Yes, sir, I do.'

Syntax, unmoving, looked deep into his eyes. Then at last he said, crisply, 'Good!'

'Sir?'

'Whatever it is you're doing, it's getting – *results*! So keep – well, yes, keep (pause) keep *doing* it!'

Syntax sped back to report to Lastrade while Kane went to his office and pondered confusion. A questioning claw ripped at his vitals, probing deep for arteries of truth, tracing their course to the heart of decision. He found it at last in Cutshaw's arrival.

The grinning astronaut slammed his door shut, quietly locked it and moved to the desk, leaning across it and savagely rhyming. 'Twinkle, twinkle, "Killer" Kane! How I wonder whom you've slain! Bet you thought I'd never get here!'

Kane replied like a snarling leopard. 'Can it, bright

144

eyes! Can the sermon! What the hell were you up to out in formation?'

'Didn't you love it? A stirring sight! It was intended to convince you that we can be *trusted*, Colonel Caribou! That we're *dependable*! Understand? We intend to keep your secret, "Little Flower of the Nut House"!'

'Why?'

'Come, now, don't be obtuse. A favor here, a favor there. You'll be notified, dear heart.'

'So that's the deal.'

'Good! That's settled! Now then, tell me, wizard ape, how does it feel to kill with your hands?'

Kane was learning what he had feared, and anger grew with the realization. He spat, 'What's eating you, Mighty Manfred? Bugged because you'd never have the guts to do the same?'

Cutshaw grabbed at a paperweight. 'Why you crummy son-of-a—!'

Kane bolted up from his chair. 'Go on, throw it, Moon Boy, throw it! That would give me a nice excuse to tear you limb from useless limb! Come on, throw it, you little phony, and then maybe on your deathbed you can tell me how it feels to throw a moonshot down the tubes!'

'Watch your tongue, sir!'

'Watch my *foot*, sir! Who are you kidding with your nut act!'

'Well, now, Spoor, I think, is crazy.'

Kane was stunned by the tacit admission. There it was. The door was closed. 'I'm not making any deals,' he said, sick; sick at heart.

'Kane, you're *mad*! Don't you know where they'd

145

send you? Idiot, Communist guerrillas have been in-filtrating Fapistan! *Outer*most Fapistan!'

'Fine,' said Kane, 'fine. "Hud, confess!"' That's what you wanted? That's what you'll get. Because tomorrow I'm phoning the General and telling him who I am.'

'*What?!*'

'You really had me conned; had me conned all the way. I thought I could cut it; shape you up. But, Cutshaw, suddenly it's clear to me I'll *never* shape you up! You'll play Bingo here 'til *discharge* day and I'll wind up in a *basket*! You're not crazy or psychotic, you're just plain *goofing off*!'

'Look at who's calling the kettle black!' said Cutshaw.

'Yes. Yes, you're right. But I'm taking care of that tomorrow. And while I'm at it I'm telling the General that all of you are sane!'

Cutshaw leaped suddenly onto the sofa, springing from there onto the desk, bawling in frantic, desperate accents, 'Hud, you're *crazy*, we're *crazy*! Out of our *minds*! Mad! Mad!' He ripped his shirt clear down to the navel.

Kane eyed him with contempt. 'So was I ever to come here.' He strode to the door, yanked it open and went out.

Cutshaw leaped after him, raced to the door, cupped his hands to his mouth and shouted wildly: 'Shane, come back! Please, come back! Mother wants you, Shane, she needs you!' And then pitifully he wailed, 'Shaaaaannnnnnne! Come baaaaaaack!'

Corfu appeared before him, dabbing his nose with royal blue, mourning, 'Blue – the color of failure!

You have lost for us our *pigeon*!' Then Corfu felt sudden shock as he saw the expression in Cutshaw's eyes: chilling fear and desperation.

By the fall of night, Colonel Kane was drunk. At nine o'clock he emerged from his quarters, a bottle of bourbon in his hand. He walked down the stairs in rigid lurch, heading for Fell, who was in his clinic. They had been drinking together for hours. At the foot of the stairs stood Captain Groper, gently smirking as Kane approached. 'Therapy, Colonel Kane?' Without breaking stride or turning his head, Kane flicked out a hand with effortless grace. It hit Groper's arm and sent him toppling to the floor like a giant sequoia, branches crackling with incredulity. 'Shock treatment, Captain,' murmured Kane, and entered the clinic.

Fell was seated on the accountant's stool, deep in abortive effort to play the pinball machine with his feet. Kane lurched heavily up beside him. 'Fell, I'm giving you one more chance.'

'Gimme the bottle,' slurred Fell. As he reached out a hand, Kane pulled back the bottle.

'After you tell me,' said the Colonel.

Fell eyed him severely with red-grained orbs. 'Colonel Kane, have you been drinking?'

'Come on, tell me, wily medic: what do you think when you're examining a pretty girl?'

'That's a *Hippocratic secret*!'

'Final answer?'

'Final answer.'

'Then I will pray – pray on bended knees – for the advent of socialized medicine!'

'How I hate an ugly drunk,' said Fell.

'Choice. Take your choice.'

Fell's expression was that of a hippo deep in the throes of painful decision. Then, 'Okay,' he said at last, falling heavily from the stool. He walked to the examination table, sat on it, deeply resigned, then sighed and stretched out on his back. 'Okay, you win, "Killer" Kane.'

Kane had gone to him and told him after the final discussion with Cutshaw. He'd said to Fell, 'I'm "Killer" Kane.'

'I could have *told* you that, you idiot,' Fell had replied with drunken serenity. He had 'suspected all along' that Kane was certainly no psychologist. And then the subject had been dropped. Fell showed no interest, and when Kane would come back to it, Fell would deliberately try to sidetrack, as though he found the topic painful. Kane gave up. He merely drank.

'What am I thinking,' said Fell, 'when I examine a pretty girl.' Kane dragged over the stool, slowly hoisted himself upon it, so that he sat behind Fell's head in classic patient-analyst relationship. 'I try to think of elephant jokes and my vast investments in medical buildings; *never* what I'm doing.'

'Same with me,' maundered Kane. 'Same with me, same with me. Always thought of something else. Burnt-out case by Graham Greene.'

'Dammit, what in the hell are you mumbling about?'

'Why should animals suffer?'

Fell reached out after a grimace. 'Gimme the bottle; you've had enough.'

Kane ignored him – or did not hear him – as Fell

took the bottle. 'Your attitude toward women, Fell – hasn't it gotten – clinical? Tough? Unfeeling?'

'Nothing,' said Fell emphatically, 'that a change of scene hasn't cured.'

'I'd hoped the same,' murmured Kane, 'would work for me . . . for me . . . God or Caesar?' he murmured thickly. Abruptly he stared at the back of Fell's head. 'Fell, are the men all goofing off?'

'*That*,' said Fell, exasperated, 'is the twentieth time you've asked me! And the answer is the same: I don't know and I don't care!'

'You don't?'

'No, I don't. Not enough to make waves. That's the lesson I've learned in the Air Force, Kane – *don't make waves*! In a word, when you're snug, and safe and secure in a sack of horseshit, buddy, don't move!'

'I care,' murmured Kane. 'I care . . . I care.'

'For them? Or yourself?'

The clinic door burst open. Spoor bounced in with his dog. 'I'm in trouble! Big trouble!'

Fell eyed him blankly. 'Take two aspirin,' he advised, 'and call my service in the morning.'

Kane slipped off the stool, moved to the pinball machine and played. The sight of an inmate was unbearable.

Spoor advanced on Fell. 'Captain, the problem isn't medical! It's purely motivational!'

'In that case, I can help you,' said Fell nipping at the bottle.

But Spoor swooped over to Kane. 'Colonel Kane, I speak of Hamlet and the problem of his madness! I am having quite an argument, and maybe you can *help*!'

'Oh?' said Kane.

'Yes, *oh*! Look, some say Hamlet's really nuts. Am I right? Am I right? Sure! But other Shakespearean scholars insist that Hamlet's just *pretending*; that he's putting on an *act*. Now I come to you as a colonel, as a lover of the Bard and a sympathetic pussycat. What is *your* opinion?'

Kane recalled that Spoor was the inmate named by Cutshaw as truly demented. 'I don't know,' said Kane. 'What's yours?'

'Lovely man!' exclaimed Spoor, leaping nimbly onto the machine so that the glass beneath him shattered. Spoor blithely ignored it, rattled onward with his theory. 'I think it's a combination! See? First, look at what Hamlet does. Just for *openers* he walks around the palace in his *underwear*! Then he calls the king his "*mother*"; tells his mother she's a *slut*; tells a nice old man he's *senile*; throws a tantrum at a *theater* party; almost jumps the *girl*! And what filthy things he *says* to her! Now then – is he crazy?'

Fell said, '*Sure*, he's crazy, idiot.'

Spoor said, '*Wrong!*'

'What?'

'*Wrong!* Look, I'll agree he's got a reason. Sure, 'cause first his father dies, and then his girl leaves him flat and then his father's ghost *appears* to him and tells him he was *murdered*! And by *whom*? By Hamlet's *uncle*, whom his mother recently *married*! Now those are pretty tough potatoes for a high-strung *kid*! For a sensitive *youth*! They're enough to drive him crazy! I mean, especially if you consider that all this happened in very cold *weather*!'

'That's what I *said*,' said Fell. 'He's crazy.'

'No, he's *not*! He's *pretending*! But if Hamlet hadn't pretended, then he *would* have gone crazy! Acting nutty is a *safety* valve!'

Kane, for the first time, looked at Spoor, a flicker of interest in his eyes. 'Let's have that again?'

'Pay attention! Look – Hamlet isn't psycho. But he's hanging on the *brink*! A little *push*, a little *shove* and the kid is *gone*, hear me, *gone*! So his *sub*conscious mind makes him do what keeps him *sane* – namely, acting like he's *not*! Acting nutty is a *safety* valve! A way to let off *steam*! A way to get rid of your *aggressions*, and all your *fears*, and all your *guilts* and all your heaven knows what *else*!'

Kane echoed 'guilts', in an odd tone of voice.

'Guilts! Yes, *guilts*!' repeated Spoor. 'And he knows that it's *safe*, understand me, *safe*! If *I* did what Hamlet does in the *play*, they'd lock me *up*! Put me *away*! But Hamlet gets away with it! And *why*, I ask you, *why*? 'Cause he knows that nuts are not responsible! He can get away with murder! Listen, let's not get into that; that's *another* hangup *al*together!'

'Does Hamlet think that he's crazy?' asked Kane.

Spoor eyed him with pity. 'Does a crazy man *ever*?'

'No,' said Kane; 'no.'

'Well, neither does Hamlet,' insisted Spoor. 'And notice – the crazier he acts in the play, why, man, the healthier he gets!'

'What?'

'The crazier he acts, Colonel, the *healthier* he gets! Now, then, tell me, Colonel Pussycat – do you or don't you agree?'

'I think I do,' murmured Kane.

'Hah!' Spoor leaped down from the pinball machine

and pointed at his dog. 'There! *Now* do you believe me,' he crowed, 'you temperamental idiot!' Spoor looked up at Kane. 'Thank you, *thank* you, Colonel Pussycat! You'll have house seats opening night!' Spoor glided out of the office.

Cutshaw was waiting in the dorm. 'Did he buy it?' he pounced on Spoor.

'Did he *buy* it? Listen, *I* bought it! *I* think something's *wrong* with us!'

'We've got him!' exulted Cutshaw. 'Now we pull out all the stops! We'll drive him crazy just convincing him that *we're* crazy! Got it?'

'Don't you get it?' Kane demanded.

Fell's voice was bleakly cynical. 'Man, they'll try *anything* to keep you from telling the General they're goofing off. They'd have to *leave* this little paradise.'

'You don't understand,' said Kane, exhilarated.

'It's a *con*!' Fell insisted. 'They dug up that Hamlet junk from your textbooks, man! Hell, haven't you read them?'

'*Desperation* dug up that theory! You think they're shamming? So do *they*! Because they can't admit to *themselves* that they're sick! But they are! They're on the brink! These men are Hamlet down the line! And obviously desperate enough to dig up the cure and lay it right in my lap!'

'Cure?'

'The crazier they act,' said Kane, 'the healthier they'll get! I'm going to stay! I'm going to stay! I'm going to indulge their wildest whims!' Kane's head was whirling with visions; then with schemes; then with doubts. A sudden notion slapped his face. Wasn't his 'great impersonation' just as mad an indulgence as Hamlet's? as Cutshaw's? as Zook's? My God, he thought, even madder, madder than Spoor's or any of the others! Kane thought he heard a cry of piercing agony from afar; a cry of terror; a cry for help. Then he realized, with sudden horror, why the voice that went on shrieking was so achingly familiar; the voice was his own.

Fell caught him as he fainted.

CHAPTER ELEVEN

Fell carried Kane up to bed. As the medic was pulling up the blanket, Kane opened his eyes. 'Does Groper know?' he murmured.

'No,' answered Fell.

Kane closed his eyes again and slept. Fell looked down at him sadly, felt his pulse, then left the room.

Kane dreamed. And this time remembered. Although later he wasn't sure that it was a dream; that it hadn't happened. He thought he'd abruptly opened his eyes and seen Captain Cutshaw sitting beside him, smoking a cigarette by his bed. Kane said, 'What? What do you want?'

'It's about my brother, Lieutenant Spoor. You've got to help him.'

'Help? How?'

'Leslie Spoor is possessed of a devil, Hud, and I want you to cast it out. He is levitating nightly and it's upsetting Lieutenant Zook. It reminds him of his belt. Also, Spoor talks to dogs, which is not entirely natural. I want you to exorcise him tonight. You're a colonel and a Catholic and an unfrocked priest. It's your *duty*, Colonel No-Face!'

Kane said, 'I can't!'

'You mean, you *won't*!'

'I mean I *can't*! I don't know how! I really want to, but I can't! I've forgotten how to do it!'

'All you have to do is care. Then you'll remember,' Cutshaw told him.

Suddenly Spoor was in the room floating three feet off the floor. He was wearing a high-altitude flight suit. He looked at Kane and opened his mouth and out came the yappings of a dog.

Kane put a finger to his neck and felt a round Roman collar. He was a priest! It was true! He was a priest after all! He felt a surging exhilaration; felt a release; felt a joy. It was the feeling after confession that had long been postponed; that had long been feared and dreaded. He lifted an arm and pointed at Spoor. 'Satan,' he commanded, 'be gone! In the name of Christ Jesus!'

Spoor continued to levitate. He grinned evilly at Kane. Then he rasped, 'You don't care.'

'Yes, I *care*!'

'But not for yourself.'

Kane remembered what was wrong. He should have asked the demon his name. 'I adjure you in the name of Christ, in the name of the living God, demon, to tell me who you are!'

Spoor's tongue lolled out of the side of his mouth, red and narrow and long. 'Call me Legion, for we are many. We are eighty-two plus one.'

'Who is the one?' asked Kane, knowing.

' "Killer" Kane!' said Spoor, and vanished.

It was then that the dream changed in texture, seemed to be not a dream at all. Cutshaw was staring at him intently, his cigarette glowing in the darkness. 'You awake?' said the apparition.

Kane moved his lips, tried to say 'Yes', but no sound

would issue forth. He spoke with his mind, thinking – saying? – 'Yes.'

'Do you really believe in an afterlife?'

'Yes.'

'No, come on. I mean, *really*.'

'Yes, I believe.'

'Tell me why.'

'I just know.'

'Blind faith?'

'No, not that; not that, exactly. Although it *is* partly feeling.'

'Then how do you *know*?' insisted Cutshaw.

Kane paused, dredging for arguments. Then at last he said (thought?), 'Because every man who has ever lived has been born with desire for perfect happiness. But unless there is an afterlife, fulfillment of this desire is a patent impossibility. Perfect happiness, in order to be perfect, must carry with it the assurance that the happiness won't cease; that it will not be snatched away. But no one has ever had such assurance; the mere fact of death serves to contradict it. Yet why should Nature implant – universally – desire for something that isn't attainable? I can think of no more than two answers: either Nature is consistently mad and perverse, or after this life there's another; a life where this universal desire for perfect happiness can be fulfilled. But nowhere else in creation does Nature exhibit this kind of perversity; not when it comes to a basic drive. An eye is always for seeing and an ear is always for hearing. And any universal craving – that is, a craving without exception – has to be capable of fulfillment. It can't be fulfilled *here*; so it's fulfilled, I think, somewhere else; some*time* else. Does that make any sense at all? I think I'm dreaming, so it's hard.'

Cutshaw's cigarette glowed bright. 'Why did Nature make fleas and dinosaurs? Or putting it your way, why did Foot?'

'I don't know,' responded Kane. 'But the concepts aren't analogous. In the first case, you see, we have all the pieces of the puzzle; or at least as much of the data as seems to bear upon the problem. But in the second we're merely speculating on causes and motives unknown. We don't know why Nature – or God – created dinosaurs or fleas. Yet we concede that there *might* be a reason which is not yet quite apparent; such as a necessary condition for the evolution of man. Why did God make the planet Mars? To me, it's senseless and superfluous. But I might change my mind about that when you get there.'

There followed a very extended pause. Cutshaw's cigarette tip flared briefly, and at last he spoke in a whisper. 'Kane, you sadistic bastard!'

Then Cutshaw was gone. Kane closed his eyes. Or ceased to dream – he didn't know which. He thought he saw Cutshaw in the room again that night, and asked him, 'Are you crazy?' Cutshaw answered him immediately: 'I don't know.' And again was gone.

Kane awakened, but not in bed. He was sitting on the floor in a corner of the room. He could not fathom how he had gotten there. He remembered fainting, remembered the dream. And remembered he'd come to some shocking awareness only seconds before he'd fainted. What it was, he couldn't recall. Nor did he feel inclined to try. He dressed in his blues and went to his office. It was only four A.M.

Kane flipped psychology books from his shelves, skimming rapidly for some reference that would tend to confirm his theory. By dusk he'd not found it. But then he noticed a title was missing. And he remembered – *Madness in Hamlet*. Faintly, he smiled. And knew he was right. Kane leaned back in his chair, lit a cigarette and relaxed. Smoke curled up from the cigarette as he looked, with remembered affection, at the pied beauty of dawn. Sunrise and sunset, he'd loved them as a boy. They had filled him with a sense of glory, made him feel somehow closer to God; a God he could touch, and see and breathe. 'Peace I leave you, My peace I give you . . .' He remembered the words from the Mass and wondered what had happened to that peace. Then tried to forget the answer. His glance scanned the wood that hemmed in the courtyard. Trees turning bare; birds singing fitfully, flitting from branch to branch. Suddenly, he thought he detected movement somewhere deep inside the wood; something that looked like a woman, again, a woman gowned in black. But when he stared at the figure directly, he saw nothing, nothing at all. Am I in the madhouse, wondered Kane, or is the madhouse in me?

He thought once more of his theory, and was vaguely nagged by a formless feeling that the theory somehow related to him. He deliberately refused to pursue it. But from time to time, as he brooded, putting an ear to the sounds of awakening, he found himself thinking of Gregory Peck. He irritably wondered why.

159

Cutshaw came in at seven, irrupting unannounced in his customary fashion. 'Good morrow, Killer Cat!' he blared. 'I've come to help you pack!'

'That won't be needed,' answered Kane.

'Think I'd demand a tip, you swine? Fie, fie on your couth!'

'I'm not leaving.'

'You're not *what*?' Manfred Cutshaw feigned surprise as though his life depended upon it.

'I'm not leaving. I've changed my mind.'

'Hud, don't tease!'

'No. You win.' Colonel Kane feigned quiet anger as though his life depended upon it. 'Go ahead. Gloat all you want. But every day away from the jungle is another day of heaven. What's the price? Name your deal!'

'Hud, don't *rush* me! Please! Don't *rush* me! Foot! Can't a man have a moment to *weep*?'

'Come on, come on! What's the price?'

'Hud, you know nothing of gracious living.'

'And you know nothing of simple honesty. Now name it, Cutshaw, name it! Name the price!' demanded Kane.

'So ridiculously modest that you'll lick my hand appreciatively. I wouldn't ask for a *thing*, in fact, but as Social Director and Games Leader I *must* provide the men with their minimal needs for self-expression.' He whipped out a paper from his pocket, began to unfold it with loving care. 'The preliminary list of particulars, Hud!'

'Come on, come on! Let's hear it!'

'Yes! First on the agenda – Spoor is ready to cast!'

'Cast?'

Cutshaw looked vaguely frimmled. 'If I were looking for an echo, Hud, I'd go to Grand Canyon. I said "Cast!", dummy, "Cast!". Spoor has finished *Julius Caesar*!'

CHAPTER TWELVE

General Syntax, on the telephone, paused for a look at the mouthpiece, not quite believing he'd heard correctly. Then he continued talking to Kane, making mysterious penciled notes on a yellow pad beside the phone.

He said, 'Dalmatians, wolfhounds, chows, and – and *what*? . . . Pekinese. Uh-huh . . . No, no, that's – no . . . I understand, that's sort of – well – yes – *therapy*. I mean, you clearly know what you're *doing*. You're – well – I've seen, you know, and Lastrade (pause) Lastrade has given carte *blanche*. You – what? . . . No, no, no, no. That's very (pause) *easy*. No. The Superman suit we can make, but the – well, the pulleys and paints. Why do you need the pulleys and paints? . . . Oh. Oh, I see. He wants to do the Slovik ceiling like the Sistine . . . *Chapel*. Yes. Now what about the flying belt? There's an experimental model or two, but they aren't too easy to get, you see, and . . . Oh? T-Tinker Bell? You're doing a performance of *Peter* (pause) *Pan*. Well, it's – look – won't he sort of – well – sort of fly over the *wall*? . . . Oh. Oh, I see. He – he promised he wouldn't *do* that . . .'

Six days later Captain Groper gripped the second-story balustrade with unbelieving hands. He had eyes but would not see; he had ears but would not hear – not the creaking of the pulleys nor the scaffold heaving before him, bearing Corfu and buckets of paint ever upward toward the ceiling like an obscene and mad benediction. Corfu, stirring paint, looked with bemusement at the Captain. '*Buon giorno*, Captain Frogface!' he greeted him as he passed.

From below came the yapping of dogs. Groper looked down at an office near Kane's. Tethered outside it, with Krebs standing guard, was a yipping, howling, barking clot of dogs of various breeds. Kane stepped out of his office, munching a sandwich with nonchalance, just as the door beside the mound of dogs flew open, revealing Spoor. He gestured into the office, commanded, 'Out! You hear me? Out!'

A rather large chow padded despondently out of the room. Spoor called angrily after him, 'And tell your stupid agent not to waste any more of my time!'

Kane stepped in to him, chewing. Spoor eyed him with outrage. 'Can you imagine? He *lisps*! Here I am casting *Julius Caesar* and they send me a dog who *lisps*!' Then he turned and called into the room, 'Alterman! *Out!* Hear me? *Out!*'

Out came Captain Alterman. He wore grieving disappointment and a blue-and-red 'Superman' costume. 'But *why*?' he pouted. '*Why?*'

Spoor looked plainly exasperated, but tried to lower his voice. 'Colonel Kane, do me a favor,' he said; 'a small but important favor. Kindly explain to this idiot that in the plays of William Shakespeare there can be no part for *Superman*!'

'There *could* be!' pouted Alterman. 'There could be, the way I explained it.'

'The way you *explained* it!' erupted Spoor. He whirled on Kane. 'Know what he *wants*? Do you *know*? When the conspirators pull out their knives, he

164

wants to *rescue* Julius *Caesar*! Sure! Swoop down and grab him! Yes! Hurdling mighty temples at a single, incredible bound! Alterman, what in the hell is *wrong* with you? *Tell* him, Colonel, *tell* him!'

'Can't be done,' said Kane to Alterman in a matter-of-fact tone of voice.

'What a pussycat!' beamed Spoor, patting the colonel's cheek with affection. Then he swiftly turned on Alterman. 'See, you stubborn? Eh? Do you see? Also, stupid, you're not a dog!'

Paint splattered down on the trio. Lieutenant Spoor pointed up at Corfu, who was busily brushing away. 'That man is *crazy*!' he declared.

Zook pounced on Kane. 'So *there* you are,' he said angrily, 'invisible giant brain!'

Spoor shook his head with sadness. 'Another planet heard from. Krebs,' he called, 'who's next?' A large Dalmatian raced into his office. Spoor followed him in and closed the door, muttering, 'Television actors! Always in a hurry!'

Kane turned to Zook. 'What's the trouble?' he calmly asked him.

'Hell, you *know* the trouble! You *caused* the trouble! Pretend to give me the belt and then one of your stooges takes it away!'

Kane had procured for him the flying belt. Developed by the Army, it was worn like a shoulder harness and could propel a man in the air for a space of from three to four minutes at most. After that, it required recharging. Its guidance system, fortunately, was simple and safe to manage.

Kane turned to Alterman, the candidate most likely

to have pilfered the belt from Zook. 'Captain, did you take the belt?'

'No, not *him*!' interjected Zook. 'It was the brain you all call Bemish! Yeah, he *robbed* it from me! *Stole* it! And for *what*, I ask you, *what*? To take a flying leap at *walls*! I want it *back*, you hear me, *back*!'

All of them looked to the door on hearing a muffled yelp of pain. Out, then, raced the Dalmatian, almost bowling over Zook. Spoor was at the door, looking outraged and chagrined. He was also gripping his wrist. 'He *bit* me! Can you imagine? Told him he was rotten and he *bit* me!' Spoor shook a threatening fist at the dogs. 'Maybe instead I'll use *penguins*! You hear, you little bums? I said *penguins*; yes, *penguins*! A penguin never bit *nobody*!'

Bemish flew past them, wearing Zook's belt. He was four feet off the ground, and how he zoomed, and how he hurtled, until a plastery crash and crunching announced the terminal point of his flight to be a staunchly resisting wall. Krebs raced to his aid, followed by Fromme, who'd burst out of the dorm.

Zook raced to the spot, bawling, 'Bemish, take it off!'

Bemish lay sprawled on the ground, his sturdy helmet white with plaster. Fromme stood over him, pushing at Krebs and shouting, 'Back! You vultures, stand back! Give the man air! Give the man air!'

Groper had seen enough. He went to his room and closed the door. Then lay on his bed and counted the years until he'd be eligible for retirement. It seemed a long, long time.

Kane entered his office feeling giddy and elated; felt

that wash of airy freedom that accompanies decision and the following of a plan. Beyond the completion of that plan he could not see; nor did he care to. It was sufficient to be moving forward, to be reaching for something palpable. And good. That was important, very important: he was striving, with maximum hazard, for something clearly and obviously good; not merely by Caesar's standards or by God's, but by both. By both. Very important. Something else was very important; some haunting, ultimate end hovering over all of the others, making them somehow intermediate. But still, he couldn't remember.

Outside, it began to rain. Kane thought back to that night in the jungle, to that night of his wild decision. Something back there. Or in a dream. He didn't know; he didn't know. *Domine non sum dignus.* Sunday mornings at the altar, holding the cruets for the priest. He felt an aching, poignant yearning for some end that was out of sight. *Agnus Dei, qui tollis peccata mundi, dona nobis pacem.* What was today? Was it Saturday? Tomorrow he'd go to Mass. Early, when it was quiet; no squalling babies rending his peace. Abruptly, without reason, he wanted to laugh; then to cry. But he knew himself incapable.

Cutshaw burst in on him, wrapped from head to foot in a gaudily striped towel. He clutched a child's pail and shovel. 'Let's go to the beach!' he announced to Kane.

'That is impossible and you know it.'

'*Foot*, you're moody!'

'Moreover, it's raining.'

'*Sure*, it's raining! That's the *point*, you dummy, the *point*! Judas, *everyone* goes when it's *bright*!'

'Is going to the beach some new demand?' asked Kane.

'Since *when* have I made demands!' squawked Cutshaw, leaping onto the couch. He slapped his shovel against the wall. 'By the way, have you fixed this freaking wall?'

'No.'

'See? Do you hear me complaining? I want a sucker,' he demanded plaintively.

'A *what*?'

'A sucker! A common sucker! Is that wrong? Is it a sin?'

'Cutshaw, kindly come down off that couch.'

'So! Once a priest, *always* a priest! Well, what is the use in goodness, Hud, if I cannot have a sucker! You're Anthony Quinn or Jack Palance! There isn't a *chance* that you're Pat O'Brien! Pat O'Brien would have given me candy! Yes! Pat O'Brien would have given me *suckers*!'

'Captain, I'll give you a sucker tomorrow.'

'Hell, I don't want one. Think you can bribe me? Listen, how do you like this towel?'

'Where did you get it?'

'Pat O'Brien. Any further idiot questions, Hud? Or did that one win the prize?'

'No further questions,' said Kane.

'Thank Foot! Want to play jacks?'

'No.'

'*Christ*, you don't want to do *anything*! What about riddles? Can I ask you a riddle?'

'Yes.'

'Big freaking deal! Now listen to this. Are you ready?' asked Cutshaw.

'Yes, Yes, I'm ready.'

'What is red, reads the New York *Times*, has fourteen legs and wears a sombrero?'

'I give up.'

'Took you *long* enough! I gave up on that one three *days* ago, Lothar! Now listen, here's another. How many times can you break a shish kebab skewer in half?'

'How many times?' answered Kane.

Cutshaw leaped from the couch, springing nimbly onto the desk in his customary fashion and squatting in front of Kane. 'I'll put it another way,' he said. 'Everything has parts. The *skewer* has parts. Now, how many times can I break it in half? An infinite number of times or a limited number of times? If it's an *infinite* number of times, then the skewer must be infinite. Which is moose piss, let's face it. But if I can only cut the skewer in half for a *limited* number of times – if I get down to a piece of skewer that can no longer be cut in half – I mean, assuming I were Foot and could do anything I wanted – then I'm down to a piece of skewer that has no parts – no parts at all; that is absolutely simple. And Hudkins, *that* is moose piss! If it has no parts, it can't *exist*! Am I right? Am I right? No! I see it in your eyes! You think I'm a crazy old man!'

'Not at all,' responded Kane. He found the problem rather intriguing. 'You have merely failed to distinguish,' he said, 'between the real and mental orders. Mentally – or theoretically – there isn't any limit at all on how many times you can halve that skewer. But in the *real* order of things – or, in other words, practically speaking – you would finally come to a point where, when you cut the skewer in half, the halves would convert themselves into energy.'

'*Foot*, you are wise!' breathed Cutshaw, probing Kane's eyes with a look like hope. He's been testing me, Kane decided. 'Do you believe in the Resurrection?' asked the astronaut intently.

'Yes,' answered Kane.

'That Christ rose from the dead?'

'Yes.'

'But the guards might have fallen asleep while cunning caribou stole his body!'

'Pilate was warned of that possibility,' said Kane. 'And the penalty for sleeping on duty for Roman soldiers happened to be death.'

'They could always plead insanity,' said Cutshaw, his face a mask of sobriety.

Kane's stomach muscles tightened. 'Temporary?' he probed.

Something stirred in Cutshaw's eyes: something vaguely like a smile. 'Maybe,' he said. 'Maybe.' Then he fell into another temper. 'Enough of these quips and quiddities! To the matter, Hud, the matter! Sir, I speak of Captain Fell!'

'What about him?'

'What *about* him? Are you *mad*? Are you a *stone*?'

'Are you referring to his drinking?'

'I'm referring to his general coolth as well as a certain lack of class! Lieutenant Klenk came to him yesterday with a strange and wondrous malady, but do you know what that quack prescribed? *Aspirin*, Huddy, *aspirin*!'

'What was the malady?'

'I blush to say it.'

'Say it.'

'Very well, I will. Lieutenant Klenk has a tipped uterus.'

'I see.'

'I daresay you do. But how does that help Lieutenant Klenk? How does that comfort him in his agony? What shall I tell him? "Listen, Klenkie, easy – I have spoken to the Colonel and, while his kidney doubtless pulsates sympathetically with yours, he says to stuff your uterus with aspirin, seeing as Fell is erratic but fair?" Is that the drill? Is that what I tell him?'

'Not at all.'

'Let's go to the beach.'

'Cutshaw, it's raining.'

'Tell that to Klenk and see if it comforts him. Look, why can't we talk? Why can't we be friends?'

'I *am* your friend,' said Kane.

'You're my *albatross*, my *millstone*, my *flaming white elephant*! Tell me, why! Why won't you tell me!'

'Tell you what?'

'Why sometimes I cry. It's a pain in the ass.'

'Yes, it is,' murmured Kane.

'That's why I love you. You're so freaking agreeable. Do you think cannibals think they're grand?'

'What?'

'Cannibals, Hud, cannibals! Do they think it's morally right to fricassee Martin and Osa Johnson?'

'Who is to say?' answered Kane.

'But it could be they do? Isn't that right?'

'Right.'

'But Foot – what about him? Does he think fricasseed hunter is grand?'

'No.'

'So how come he hasn't gotten out the word to all those cannibals, Hud? And to those pygmies shrinking heads out there in the jungles of the Amazon? What is it with him? What is it? Is he indifferent to right and wrong? Is he indifferent to what we do?'

'He sends missionaries there,' said Kane.

'He should send meat sauce and chutney, Hud; that the cannibals would use! Look, if Foot has some plan; if there's some way he wants us to act, why, man, all he'd have to do is tell us! If we were convinced that he existed – really convinced – we'd all be good. So why the games and hocus-pocus? Why doesn't Foot just make an appearance on top of the Empire State Building? What's the problem, Hud? What is it? Is he short on tablets of stone? My Uncle Eddie owns a quarry, I can get them for him wholesale! All he has to do is *ask*! A burning bush is something else. This is not my regular work.'

'I gather you're asking for signs and wonders,' said Kane.

'I'm asking for a modicum of honesty! For Foot to quit playing peek-a-boo! To shit or get off the pot! Diarrhetic strange gods have been waiting in line!'

Kane sighed. 'Do you know the New Testament?'

'Do you know you're a fatuous pedant?'

'The parables of Christ are neither simple,' said Kane, 'nor direct. Christ always has to explain them. But you'll notice he only explains them to the few who hang around; to the few who are interested; to those of goodwill. And there's a reason for that, Cutshaw.'

Cutshaw leaned forward in exaggerated interest, his

172

brow thick with furrows of intense concentration.

Kane continued: 'To those who are *not* of good-will, well – the truth can be harmful. As long as there is doubt, there is a lessening of guilt. But to give the truth to those who will believe it – but ignore it – is to seal their final damnation. I believe that's why God hides. What do you think?'

Cutshaw blinked. 'I think you are late for your tea party, you demented March Hare! Who do you claim to be today? Father Divine or Cassius Clay? Look, forget it, Hud, forget it! Stay Gregory Peck! At least you can vote!' Cutshaw flung a corner of towel over his shoulder and strode to the door. He pulled it open and turned to Kane. 'One more thing,' he said, 'I love you. You're so dumb you're adorable.' He falconed out the door then, crouching out of sight.

Kane felt a sense of failure; that he had somehow failed Cutshaw; somehow failed himself. This constant harping on theology seemed related to his problem. How lucid he was when he spoke of it! And halving the skewer of shish kebab. Testing, thought Kane, he was testing. Testing my intellect, apparently. Why? To what purpose? Would he feel better if Albert Einstein believed in Christ and the Resurrection?

Fell interrupted his thoughts, looking in to see how he felt.

'Fine,' said Kane. 'Fine.'

'Still believe in your theory?'

'Yes. I do.' Was there a choice? Kane wondered. Fell left him, looking skeptical. And Kane once more felt discouraged; felt harried by the pressure of time; nagged by the threat of discovery by the Air Force,

173

which was inevitable, he knew. If he could only cure them first. He heard the distant yapping of dogs and felt vaguely reassured. He hoped for new demands from Cutshaw; hoped they would be outrageous. The crazier, the healthier . . . faster . . . faster.

One hour later, Cutshaw returned, demanding that Kane take him with him to Mass. 'Tomorrow morning, Hud, at sunrise, when there are spirits walking abroad!'

'You're not permitted off the grounds,' said Kane.

'Hah! The truth slips out! So you are Antichrist, you filth! Or at the least, possessed of a devil!'

With a chilling start, Kane remembered his dream. Or was it a dream? But of course! Was he mad? It was a – 'Cutshaw, you believe in possession?'

'Yes. You, for example, are clearly possessed by Rebecca of Sunnybrook Farm! For heaven's sake, call an exorcist! I can't stand it another minute!'

'I'm serious. Do you believe?'

'Yes!' Cutshaw leaned forward intently. 'Foot gives no signs and wonders, Hud, but Satan is no such miser! No! Old men stabbed in a subway for laughs! A teen-age kid kills his parents with a shotgun! A father heaves his baby against a wall, crushes his head, because the kid wet his bed! Three kids from wealthy families kill a fisherman for his rowboat! Shall I go on? Shall I talk about war? Isn't *that* some kind of possession? And what of the million ways and tools devised to torture a man 'til he screams! Sometimes for kicks, Hud, just for kicks! Man, I believe! I believe in possession! I believe because devils keep doing commercials! Hell, maybe Foot hasn't heard of TV! Take me to Mass!' ended Cutshaw irrelevantly.

Kane said, 'Why do you want to go?'

'I have a deep and trenchant interest in the study of primitive cults. Also, I love to worship statues, so long as I don't have to look at their feet. They're always bare. Have you noticed? Listen, I've *got* to go, I've *got* to! I'll be marvey good, I swear it! Hud, I'll just sit and think pious thoughts!'

Kane was silent, considering.

'Okay, fronds! Can I think of fronds? What about fronds? What's the harm?'

Kane agreed to take him. He wasn't quite sure why.

That night, Kane went to confession at an A-frame wooden church in the canyon, not far from the beach. He was the last one in the church. When Kane stepped out of the confessional, kneeling to say his penance, his confessor, who was the pastor, stepped out of the box and eyed Kane strangely. Then he proceeded to read his Office, pacing slowly at the back of the church. As Kane was leaving, his hand in the holy water, the old priest paused and smiled. He asked Kane where he was stationed, and if he would like a cup of coffee. Kane went with him to the rectory and spoke to the old man for hours.

He told him something about himself; about Cutshaw and his problem: God on the Empire State Building. The priest had no answer. 'A mystery,' he murmured, 'a mystery.' Kane asked if he had any books that dealt with diabolical possession. The priest said 'Yes,' and took from his shelf a book called *Satan*. He told Kane to take it with him.

175

'Do you believe in possession, Father?'

'Fifty thousand Black Masses are said in Paris every year,' the priest replied. 'A man steals a Host that he thinks is God and horribly desecrates it. Either the man is mad or he is possessed. Who knows? Maybe possession *is* madness. If he thinks the Host *isn't* God, why take the trouble to steal it? Any old crust should do well enough.'

'Have you ever *seen* an exorcism?'

'Yes,' said the priest. 'Yes. Once in Ohio. Akron, Ohio. The possessed was levitating. I saw it. Uneducated boy, only an eighth-grade education, but he conversed in Latin and Greek.'

'He might have picked it out of the brain of the exorcist,' said Kane.

'Yes, the Church is well aware of that. Telepathy is accepted. If the possessed merely speaks in a language that is known by someone else present, that is no longer regarded as positive sign of a diabolical presence. Same with levitation. Here, the book. Let me have it a moment.'

Kane handed him the book. The priest flipped pages, stopped and read: ' "Before the priest undertakes an exorcism, he ought diligently to enquire into the life of the possessed, into his condition, reputation, health and other circumstances; and should talk them over with wise, prudent and instructed people, since the too credulous are often deceived, and melancholics, lunatics, and persons bewitched often declare themselves to be possessed and tormented by the devil: and these people nevertheless are *more in need of a doctor than of an exorcist.*" ' The priest looked at Kane. 'That was a warning to exorcists once published by the

Church. Can you guess when it was put out?'

'Rather recently, I should think.'

The priest said, 'Fifteen hundred and eighty-three.' He handed back the book. 'Here, read it. Better than horror films on The Late Show.'

Kane thanked him and left with the book. That night, the priest said a prayer for him.

The following morning just before seven, Kane sat waiting in his staff car, having sent Krebs to go and fetch Cutshaw. When the astronaut finally appeared he was wearing a clean khaki uniform, stiff with starch. His hair was thick with vaseline and his face was cleanly shaven. But he still wore his sneakers and his tattered college blazer, and affected a high Buster Brown collar tied with a bright red bow. Kane at first insisted that he remove the collar and sneakers, but relented when Cutshaw argued. 'What does Foot care about clothes!' They drove to the church and were two minutes late.

As they stepped out of the staff car, Cutshaw looked suddenly terrified and tightly gripped Kane's hand. He would not let go until after they'd entered.

Kane's usual pattern was to sit in a pew far back, but as he genuflected and blessed himself, he saw, with quiet horror, that the astronaut was moving like a rocket toward the front, affecting a rapid, pigeon-toed gait, listing his shoulders from side to side. At the very front pew he paused and called to Kane in a loud stage whisper: 'Hud, up here! Let's see the statues!'

Kane felt ice forming on his kneecap. He wanted to vanish, become invisible, even turn into a pillar of salt. But the habit of fourteen years asserted itself, and he made an instant decision: he followed Cutshaw to the front and knelt beside him in the pew.

Cutshaw knelt stiffly, looking piously up at the priest, the latter's hands upraised, his back to the parishioners, murmuring in Latin. For a moment Kane felt better. Then, 'Is that Oral Roberts?' he heard Cutshaw rumble huskily. The priest – it was not the pastor – jerked his head around and scruted Kane severely. Then he resumed the saying of Mass. Kane debated leaving, but feared it might cause even greater disturbance, especially if Cutshaw refused to go. Thus he made truce with his sense of sacrilege.

Cutshaw was quiet until the sermon, which concerned the Good Shepherd who was willing to 'lay down his life for his sheep.' And then, when the priest made some trenchant point, Cutshaw applauded or murmured 'Bravo!' The priest, a former missionary who'd lived most of his life in China, decided Cutshaw was inebriated and certainly no more of a nuisance than squalling infants or belching warlords. When Cutshaw applauded he raised his voice a notch and offered it up to God.

When it came time for the collection, Cutshaw loudly demanded a nickel. Kane gave him a dollar. But when the collection basket was thrust at him, Cutshaw quietly gripped it, poked his nose into it, sniffing, then abruptly waved it by. He stuck the dollar into his pocket.

Kane ruefully shook his head and regretted ever bringing him. Why? he asked himself: why? For some new insight into Cutshaw? Fear of reprisal? Was that it? Or some concern for Cutshaw's soul? He looked over at the astronaut as they knelt for the consecration. Cutshaw's hands were clasped before him as he stared up at the altar, his pixie head awash in sunlight shafting narrowly through stained glass. Where did it come from, that look of innocence? From the Buster Brown collar? He looked to Kane like a tasteful Christmas card sketch of a choir boy, done in pastels.

Cutshaw behaved with decorum through the remaining parts of the Mass, except once, during the reading of the last Gospel, when he endeavored to catch a fly.

As they walked back up the aisle, Cutshaw once more took hold off Kane's hand. Outside, on the steps, he turned to Kane and said, very simply, 'I dug it.' He said no more until the car pulled up to the door of the Slovik mansion. He looked at Kane and said in a child's voice, 'Thank you, Daddy. Thank you.'

'Why did you keep the dollar?' asked Kane.

'For suckers,' said the world-famous Moon pilot. Then leaped out of the car and Grouchoed into the mansion.

Kane, as he watched him go, felt a sudden wrench of pity. Then pity sank, like a pebble, to the bottom of some fathomless lake. He hoped the therapy was working.

CHAPTER THIRTEEN

Days of unbridled chaos swarmed through the mansion like giant ants, twitching antennae of unlikelihood. Corfu painted, Zook flew and Lieutenant Spoor's dogs prowled the mansion like mangy lions. One of them, a boxer, left his calling card steaming on Captain Groper's bed. One of the inmates found it first, and carefully labeled it: *'Brand "X."'*

For Kane, these were days of dreams, lurid nightmares strung together. He was unable to remember any of them and complained to Fell of headaches. The medic, whose unexplained absences were growing increasingly frequent, administered aspirin in massive doses. The headaches did not abate. Nor did Spoor's persistent reports, at which the men invariably hissed, of seeing a 'Lady in Black.'

Kane was depressed when the men became bored. He had hoped for some massive outrage that would hasten the men's catharsis. Cutshaw continued to beard him, mostly on questions of philosophy, but he sensed some loss of momentum. Then Cutshaw made fresh demands. Elated, Kane phoned Syntax (who had been calling every day) and requested fresh logistics.

Syntax stared into the phone. 'They – they want to play "Great Escape"!' he yipped. 'Look, now, why do they? . . . Oh. It's (pause) *therapy* and . . . Yes, I understand . . . No, no, no! I agree! You cannot dig tunnels without (pause) tunneling *equipment*. But why – why the motorcycle? . . . Oh, I see. He wants to play Steve

... McQueen! Just like the movie, same as the movie ... No, no, no, Kane, I'm with it! I know that's (pause) *psychology*. But, uh, I, uh, I was a flier, you know and – well, tell me again: why the Nazi uniforms? ...'

Within a week, Captain Groper was echoing the General. He stood in the main hall, wearing an SS uniform, a snarling German shepherd dog pulling taut the leash in his hand. More in wonder than in outrage, he asked, 'Why the Nazi uniforms?'

The entire staff was wearing them. And that included Kane, who answered Groper academically: 'It's a standard tool of therapy, Captain. The patients act out some basic fear or bugaboo, and this provides catharsis and social relearning. Very elementary. It's known as "Psychodrama."' Kane started to spell it for him, but Groper interrupted.

'I know how to *spell* it, sir. But *why the Nazi uniforms?*'

'Realism, Captain, realism. There's no therapy at all unless the drama seems real. The inmates are playing a part – they're playing the part of Allied prisoners who are tunneling to freedom from a camp in Nazi Germany. *We* are playing a part – we are pretending to be their captors.'

Paint splattered down on them. Corfu had refused to play, preferring, instead, to continue painting. Kane and Groper looked up; then quickly down again on hearing the roar of an engine. Lieutenant Fairbanks, riding a motorcycle, burst through the mansion front doors. Kane and Groper leaped backward as Fairbanks zoomed directly between them, making a handsome but abortive effort to run the cycle up the staircase.

'We are their captors,' murmured Groper, as he stared at Fairbanks, mesmerized. Then Spoor irrupted before him, throwing his arms around the dog and shouting, 'Marc Antony, I've found you!'

The blasting sound of jackhammers reached them from the dorm. Kane walked slowly to the dormitory door, pulled it open and looked inside. The men were sedulously ripping up the dormitory floor. Dirt, rocks and wood flew up from the hole that they were digging. Among the men was Cutshaw, holding a blueprint spread out before him. He was instructing Bemish and Zook, who were both leaning on shovels. Cutshaw shouted over the drilling: 'Now this will be Tunnel One, dug by Team One, intersecting with Tunnel Two, dug by Team Two, intersecting with Tunnel Three dug by Team Three. One and Two are decoys. Three is the big one – maximum security!'

'May we ask where they go?' said Zook.

'Yes,' answered Cutshaw proudly. 'Absolutely nowhere!' Then he caught Kane's eye and grinned. 'Heavenly Caribou, you are ours!' he shouted. 'Ours and no one else's!' Kane closed the door. And *prayed* that his theory was right.

Two weeks passed. The tunneling continued feverishly. Supports were rigged for shoring, and miniature tracks were laid, with wheeled flatboards used to ride them, shuttling men back and forth as they worked at clearing the dirt.

Around the perimeter of the courtyard, platforms were erected, massive searchlights mounted upon them. They were patroled by Krebs and Christian, rifles over their shoulders and guard dogs in leash. Once, as they approached each other from opposite ends of the platform, they paused and looked expressionlessly into one another's eyes.

'Our country, right or wrong,' said Krebs. Then both the airmen moved on, and were never observed to converse again. Although once, when it was raining, Sergeant Christian could not refrain from blurting, 'I'll bet *my* savage dog can lick *your* savage dog.' Krebs, resisting this heady wine, refused to be lured into answering. He merely went on walking, brooding on madness and its causes. He gave considerable thought to its symptoms.

Groper, during this period, quietly took to drink as well as to lengthy conversations with Sergeant Bemish on the nature of matter. He developed a habit of saying 'Fascinating!', which eventually grated on Bemish, who began sedulously to avoid him; though sometimes Groper, in his cups, would pursue him into the tunnels, muttering cosmological inanities, such as, 'Where does space end?' Once, in one of the tunnels, Bemish said, 'Groper, get off my back!' and when Groper answered serenely with '$E = MC^2$,' Bemish threw dirt into his face. Then Groper muttered 'Fascinating!', and Bemish frankly screamed.

Fell, for the most part, was missing, his room invariably locked and equally impervious to knocking. Once in a while he was seen in the clinic, and on one of these occasions Captain Groper complained of a hangover, whereupon Fell lectured him severely on the evils of 'demon rum.' He also refused him aspirin, bawling, 'Let this be a lesson, lush!' Groper felt rejected, but mumbled, 'Fell, I bear you no malice.' Fell crammed dental floss down his throat.

Kane once again was tormented by doubt; then by

184

nightmares; then by headache. Cutshaw continued his quizzes, and when he seemed lucid, Kane felt hope. Then Cutshaw would lapse once again into lunacy; or its pretense; Kane no longer distinguished. The only apparent result of Kane's therapy was an evident and increasing madness among the members of his staff. Kane began to crack. He complained to Cutshaw about the tunneling.

'Thirteen tunnels! That's enough!' he snapped, his night spent sleepless in headache.

Cutshaw drew himself erect. 'No, Colonel Streicher! The work must go on!'

'Until when?'

'Until *when*? Until the maze is completed!'

Kane wiped sweat from his forehead. His doubts had grown monstrous, Hydra-headed and hissing.

'Moreover,' continued Cutshaw, 'I must protest in the strongest terms a certain flagrant contravention of the Geneva Convention! Conditions in these tunnels are *disgraceful*, Colonel Streicher! I insist upon our rights!'

'Namely what?'

'Namely, proper toilet facilities every fifty feet of tunnel!'

Kane felt an impulse to strike him, an impulse he barely resisted; then an urge to blurt out the truth; to tell Cutshaw he knew that he was pretending. But he merely stared for a moment, then abruptly walked away. En route to his room he was mauled by a dog. Groper, who saw it happen, shook his head and said 'Fascinating!' Bemish was not there to hear it; undoubtedly a phenomenon to which Groper owed his life.

Several days later, Cutshaw was shocked when some of the inmates expressed boredom with tunneling. There was a briskness in their mood, an awareness like spring and reawakening. Then when Cutshaw saw Klenk at a window, staring up at the puffy contrails of a B-58 with an expression that might have been longing, Cutshaw grew furious and ordered him down to the tunnels. He also determined that the 'Great Escape' must move to another phase. That night he bearded Kane.

'You want to do *what*?' exclaimed Kane.

'Switch sides!' repeated Cutshaw. 'Starting this very night, Fritz, you and the staff will be inmates, see, and *we* will be the staff! Psychologists call it role-playing! But then, *you* wouldn't know.' He tossed a slim yellow folder onto Kane's desk. 'Here, study your script!'

'Script?'

'Tonight's interrogation, dunce! We'll find that new tunnel or break every one of you!' Cutshaw leaned across Kane's desk and quickly flipped to a page in the script. 'Notice, incidentally, that you crack on page two. First, you scream horribly, then—'

Fairbanks interrupted in a manner that was hard to ignore. He had zoomed into the office on his 'Steve McQueen' cycle, flipping the handlebars acrobatically so that the spinning front wheel wound up resting on Kane's desk. Cutshaw eyed him serenely. 'Shouldn't you have knocked?'

'The door was open,' said Fairbanks. Then he squeezed the cycle's horn, which emitted a raucous blast. 'Breakthrough,' announced Fairbanks, 'in Tunnel Fourteen!'

Cutshaw went down with him into the tunnels, and found that the men had intersected a concrete-lined passageway that ran beneath the mansion. Outside the opening that led into it, Zook and Bemish played gin. Cutshaw poked his head into the passageway briefly, then turned and looked at Fairbanks. 'Where does it go?'

'I dunno. Spoor's checking it out.'

Cutshaw heard a yapping from somewhere in the maze. He turned a frimmled eye on Fairbanks. 'Kindly instruct Lieutenant Spoor to keep his dogs out of the tunnels! There's slippage enough as it is!' Then he turned on Zook and Bemish. 'Idiots, up! ... No flaking off!'

'We're tired. Tired of the whole damn bit,' said Zook.

'Up, you laggards, up!' roared Cutshaw. 'Switch uniforms with the staff!' The men leaped up, for in Cutshaw's voice was a surprisingly genuine anger. Fairbanks looked at him oddly, and saw in his eyes a desperation that almost caused him to gasp in shock. He followed the others out of the tunnel.

Leslie Spoor was padding cautiously along the passageway with a flashlight, flicking its beam over bas-relief horror masks that were inset in the walls. He was not happy with his surroundings. And he felt terribly alone, Rip Torn having demurred from joining him in a manner hardly calculated to shore up his master's spirits: he had poked his snout into the passage, then scrambled backward in a frenzy, tucking his tail between his legs, and thereupon ululating horribly. Spoor had then said 'Shit!', but he had drawn the low card.

Spoor suddenly halted. The beam of his flashlight had picked up the outlines of something that looked like a door in the wall. He moved in closer, but could find no doorknob; no handle; no lever. Only a frieze of Bela Slovik in the center of the door. Spoor delicately probed with his fingers, gouging its eyes, picking its ears. When he pressed the head's nose, it depressed like a doorbell. Spoor jumped back. The door was opening, silently sliding into the wall. Flickering light snaked across Spoor's face. Then he slowly stepped into the room. And gaped in awe and amazement.

Set high on the walls, burning bright, were flaming torches that cast their light on a scene from Poe at his most intimidating. Toothy bats were strung from the ceiling, hanging by wires that were almost invisible and hovering low over lifelike wax effigies that were clearly unrelated to pop art: a hooded executioner holding his ax upraised over a kneeling, terrified victim; a severed head sitting in a bird cage, its mouth gaping in scream; a half-naked girl manacled to a zombie. Plastered all over the walls were lurid posters hawking films that Bela Slovik had once made famous. And in the center of the room, surrounded by votive candles and flowers, resting on an inclined ramp, lay a heavy, open coffin containing a lifelike effigy of Slovik.

Spoor's showmanship quelled his fears. He moved closer to the coffin, looked down at the flowers, gently plucked one and sniffed. 'Fresh!' he marveled softly. 'And who lit the candles?' He stared at the Slovik effigy. '*You*, little pussycat?'

The Slovik effigy sat up, opened its eyes and leered fiendishly. And in a rasping, horrible voice, it said: 'I love you!'

Spoor shrieked.

Kane was lacing his sneakers. He'd just traded uniforms with Cutshaw at the astronaut's insistence. Now he knotted the laces and looked in the mirror. The sleeves of the sweater were inches too short. Same with the trousers. Too short. What am I doing? Kane wondered abruptly. What's happening? What? Spasmodically, he clutched at his head, tried to smother the fire that licked at his brain. Then once more he caught his reflection. And suddenly he giggled; then began to laugh hysterically, doubling over onto the couch. Abruptly he sobered, left the office. Fell would have something strong – stronger than aspirin – for the pain. En route to the clinic, he walked past Groper, who was sitting rather despondently on the back of one of the sofas, moody head resting on a fist. He was still in Nazi uniform.

'You're out of uniform,' said Kane as he passed him.

'No one would trade with me,' Groper sulked.

The clinic was locked. Fell wasn't there. Kane stared at the door for several moments, felt paint splattering onto his head. He craned his neck at Corfu, who had almost completed his painting: destroyers and carriers cutting through waters, beneath them a massive multicolored slogan reading: *'U.S. Navy! Our first line of defense!'*

A pack of dogs, running through the hall, almost knocked Kane off his feet. Pain again, deep. He felt at a temple, throbbing, throbbing; then found himself staring at one of the canvases set up in the middle of the hall: the one of the finger pierced by a needle, dripping blood, red, red . . . Kane took the painting from its easel and carried it upstairs.

Fell lay sprawled in bed wearing gaily striped pajamas. He was examining his reflection in a gilded, ornate hand-mirror. On his head was a stiff white 'fright wig.' 'Say something in Doctor Zorba,' he mumbled, as his door lock suddenly clicked home. Fell looked up at the Lady in Black. She pulled back her veil and uttered 'Norman!'

'Consuelo!' husked Fell.

Consuelo Endicott took a flying leap at the bed, crying, 'I can only stay a minute!'

They did not answer Kane's urgent knocking.

Kane went to his quarters, set down the painting, then went in to the bathroom and washed his hands. He washed them for twenty minutes.

Cutshaw was leaning against a tree, deep in the wood that surrounded the mansion, when Spoor at last found him. He'd been there an hour, brooding on Kane; on himself; on his motives. He needed Kane, he knew that. That was his reason for sending in Spoor: to entice the Colonel into staying. He'd thought all along that he was sane, his problem wholly unrelated to that of the other inmates; he thought he'd been telling Kane obliquely how to help them; how to cure them. But what of himself? Where lay truth? He did not know. He merely suspected.

A clap of thunder turned Cutshaw's gaze upward.

Rain clouds were sweeping in angrily off the sea. He turned up the black leather collar of the SS uniform, feeling a chill; yet there was no breeze. He noticed the birds had ceased their twittering. Abruptly he smiled at a random thought. Once he had been an altar boy. What would Kane ever think of that? It began to rain.

Spoor leaped out from behind a bush. 'He's alive!'

'Who?'

'Slovik! Bela Slovik! He's alive!'

'Let go my arm,' said the moody Cutshaw.

'He's *alive*, I tell you! I *saw* him!'

'You're crazy!'

'But he spoke!'

'Spoke *what*? What did he *say*?'

'He said, "I love you!"' said Leslie Spoor.

Cutshaw shrieked and lifted an arm as though to strike a savage blow. Spoor scuttled backward, tripped on a rock, fell to his knees, recovered and ran. Cutshaw moved deeper into the wood, into the light but steady rain; deeper into himself.

Spoor pounced severally on the inmates, insisting that 'Slovik is alive!' He tried to draw them into the tunnels, and from thence into the passageway, but his efforts were rudely resisted. One of the men roundly cuffed him. At last, he shouted his claims to Corfu, who listened attentively, politely, then spilled green paint into Spoor's raving mouth.

'Medic!' bawled Spoor, then realized the ultimate futility of ever finding Fell. He cried out, 'Kane! Colonel Kane!' He raced to Kane's office, and not finding him there, rushed up the staircase and burst into his room. Kane was examining the painting of the impaled index finger. Something had been added – from the end of the needle dangled a skeleton, a rope around its neck.

'Colonel Pussycat, you've been had!' blurted Spoor, his cheeks turned red with anger.

'What?'

'*Had!* You've been *had!* All that foop about Hamlet's madness, sir! Cutshaw put me up to it! And only to get you in *trouble!* See? Merely to keep you *around!*'

'I have known for some time,' said Kane. 'The theory is nonetheless true.'

'Nuts! We're all still crazy as bedbugs! Yes! Crazier than *before!* And I demand that Cutshaw be punished! Punished *severely*, you understand? He is a toad and not at all nice! Not at all—!' Spoor abruptly noticed the painting. 'Hey, that's *mine!* That's my *painting!* Isn't it grand? Isn't it—!' He craned his neck at the painting. 'Hey, somebody *ruined* it! Who did the skeleton? What lackey destroyed my work of art?'

Kane's eyes were vague, his voice low and dim. 'Are you mad? Truly mad?'

'Yes! Except Tuesdays! Tuesdays I'm not sure!'

'And Cutshaw?'

'Out of his *mind!* Nonetheless he needs punishment! Are you going to punish him?'

Kane stared down at the painting and said, 'Yes – I am going to punish him.'

'Grand! May I be so bold as to suggest the means? Let's do *Titus Andronicus* and bake him in pie!'

Kane's telephone rang. 'Please leave,' he said to Spoor. When Spoor had gone, Kane answered the phone. It was Syntax, calling to advise that General Lastrade and Senator Hesburgh would be visiting them early the following day. Syntax asked for reassurance that the men were 'all right.'

'They're all right,' said Kane numbly. 'I guarantee – they're all right.' He hung up and murmured, 'They *will* be.'

Kane walked to the door of his room, opened it wide and looked down the hall – at the pack of yapping dogs; at Corfu on his scaffold; at Krebs in Nazi uniform; at the myriad mounds of dirt heaped beside entrances to tunnels; then at himself, in Cutshaw's clothing. He saw Fairbanks zoom out of the dormitory, trick-riding his motorcycle, and noisily hurdling a sofa. Kane summoned Krebs and informed him of the coming inspection, asked him to summon Captain Groper. Krebs reported Groper missing. He was last seen entering the tunnels and had yet to emerge.

Groper, at that moment, was at the end of the secret passageway. He'd stumbled into it by chance, while seeking Bemish for discussion. Now his fingers pressed at the surface of what seemed to be a door. He pushed, inadvertently, at the nose of a bas-relief horror mask, and the door, to his amazement, quietly slid open. He stepped into a bedroom. It was dark and unlit, but he could make out women's garments and smelled the cloying scent of sachet. He went to a door. It was locked. He turned the latch, slowly opened it. And looked into the eyes of Jane Mawr, who was standing in the girl's school corridor, about to knock on the door.

'Fascinating!' said Groper, who was still in Nazi uniform.

Miss Mawr frankly screamed.

'Do you read poetry?' asked Groper.

Miss Mawr stopped screaming, stared at him blankly. 'What?'

'Poetry – "Sweetest love, I do not go for weariness of thee . . .'?"

'John Donne!' gasped Miss Mawr.

'Yes,' said Groper. 'I'm okay.' He took her in his arms. Miss Mawr did not resist.

Cutshaw knocked at Kane's door. Getting no answer, he boldly opened it, stepped inside and closed it behind him. Then saw Kane. He sat rigidly in a chair by a large, open window, fully dressed, but apparently sleeping. A sheet of paper lay in his lap. Cutshaw moved closer, put a hand on his shoulder, intoning, 'The penalty for sleeping on duty is death! Wake up!'

Kane opened his eyes and looked at him; *through* him, with sightless eyes. 'I have never killed a lamb,' he said.

Cutshaw felt a prickling at the base of his neck. Then, suddenly he grew furious, shouting, 'Kane! Wake up! I need you!', slapping him sharply across the face.

Slowly, gradually, Kane's eyes came into focus. He said, 'Cutshaw, what do you want?' He thought that he was dreaming. When Cutshaw spoke, he heard only faintly.

The astronaut sat on the floor. 'Have you thought about my problem?'

'What problem?' asked Kane.

'Foot's refusal – if he exists – to clearly promulgate his laws.'

'The paper,' said Kane. 'Take the paper – it's there.'

The astronaut looked around, then saw the paper on Kane's lap. He picked it up, eying Kane oddly, then carefully read to himself: 'To Captain Manfred Cutshaw – I've given thought to your deepest problem; or at least, what I think is your deepest problem. And this is the closest I've been able to come to the kind of answer that might appeal to you. God knows, there are many answers, but I think you know them better than I. But this one, I believe, is different. And it is this – simply this. If a man were to appear tomorrow in the streets of New York City wearing white shining garments and possibly floating in mid-air, saying, "I am a messenger from God come to tell you clearly what He expects of you," and then said, "I'm willing to give you proof of my credentials," what do you think the reaction then would be? Of course – the people would ask for the proof. And what if they demanded, as proper proof, that the following day at precisely – *precisely* ten o'clock – the sun be made to stand still; to stand still for eighty-two minutes – not one second more, not one second less? Now, what would happen the following day if the miracle were accomplished – to the letter, to the second? Can you guess? Well, I will tell you. There would be countless explanations: coincidence, autosuggestion, mass hysteria, mass hypnosis and the like. The phenomenon would prove *nothing* – except to those who *want* to believe – to those who are men of goodwill. It has happened before; you understand that. An even greater miracle was performed. A man was raised from the dead. And then

195

another raised Himself. Many have ached – perhaps, like you – to have looked on Christ, to have touched His garments, seen the proof. As for myself, I am glad that I wasn't there. Better to doubt, better to doubt. Better to have some excuse for the blood. I hope this helps you.'

There the note ended. It was signed, 'Hudson Kane.'

Cutshaw looked up at Kane and shivered.

'I would like some cocoa now,' said the Colonel.

'Cocoa?'

'Where is Beth?'

'Who is Beth?'

Kane answered, 'My wife. Do you know her?'

'No.'

'She left me when I died.'

Cutshaw stared at Kane intently. The Colonel's eyes seemed unseeing. 'Are you awake?' Cutshaw asked softly.

'No. No, I'm dreaming. And I must try – try to remember. It's very important I remember this dream. I'm cold. Why can't I help you? Cutshaw, you really must let me help you. Brother Charles would be very ...' Here his voice trailed off.

Cutshaw waited; then said, 'I will let you help me.'

'This dream is nice. Not like the others. Why am I cold?'

Cutshaw rose. 'I'll close the window,' he said; but didn't. He merely moved to it and stared out. The rain had stopped and stars were bright.

'I would like my cocoa now.'

Cutshaw did not answer.

'Why won't you go to the Moon?'

'I'm afraid,' husked Cutshaw softly, tasting wet salt

drops on his lips. 'The stars? See the stars? How cold? How far? And lonely – very lonely. All that space; empty space – and so very far from home Kane, I've circled 'round and 'round this house – orbit after orbit – and wondered – wondered how it would be not to stop; just circle alone forever . . . up there . . . alone.' Reflected starlight shattered, gleaming, against the wetness in his eyes. 'What if I got there and couldn't get back? Everyone – dies. But I'm afraid to die alone, Kane – so very far from home. Especially if there's no God; that makes it even more horribly lonely.'

'You're not afraid,' said Kane disjointedly. 'You're just – unbalanced. I'm going to cure you. It's important. Don't worry. I will cure you.'

'I know,' said Cutshaw. 'I know.' He moved slowly to the bed, stripped off a blanket and draped it over Kane.

'This dream is nice,' said Kane, smiling. Then he leaned back his head and closed his eyes. 'I think I'll have my cocoa later . . .'

Cutshaw looked down at him for a moment, then whispered, 'God! Oh, God!' He knew that Kane was mad.

Cutshaw left and closed the door. He went downstairs and walked outside, walked into the wood to be alone.

Some of the Nazi-uniformed inmates were in the dormitory, setting up an 'interrogation room.' Spoor stood on a chair, adjusting a high-beamed, concentrated light fixture that now hung from the ceiling, newly rigged and ready for shining into some future victim's eyes. Cutshaw had earlier promised that Kane would be first to be interrogated. He was scheduled for that night.

'How's this?' asked Spoor, who had been taken back into the fold. No one else felt qualified to 'direct.'

'No,' said Zook. 'A little lower.'

'So?'

'Better. But where's the victim? Can't find *Kane*, can't find *Groper*, can't find *Fell*!'

'God will provide,' said Leslie Spoor.

At that moment a black limousine pulled up in front of the mansion door. Spoor raced to a window, saw a liveried chauffeur opening a door. Out stepped Senator Hesburgh.

'Look!' said Spoor. 'What did I tell you!'

Strong hands seized the Senator.

Lastrade was on the telephone barking at General Syntax. 'Didn't I *tell* you about that bastard? He's gone and done it – pulled a sneak! He's out at the mansion right now! Just got the word from OSI! Now, trot your fanny over there immediately! I'm on my way myself!'

Syntax hung up and ordered a staff car. He was so nervous he couldn't stammer.

Senator Hesburgh, his hands bound behind him, sat in a straight-backed wooden chair, the interrogation light in his face. His eyes were slits as he stared at Zook, who was pacing deliberately back and forth, his heavy black boots pounding the floor. Zook, affecting a German accent, said, 'We haff *ways* of making you talk, you know!'

Dully – and for the twentieth time – Hesburgh

198

chanted his outraged litany. 'I'm the United States Senator from—'

'*Silence!*' shrieked Zook. 'Give up this *pretense*! What is the *point*! Your friends have *confessed*, you idiot, *confessed*!' Then Zook adopted a gentler tone; syrupy, persuasive, as he reached for the cigarettes in his tunic pocket. 'Let me persuade you not to be foolish. Make it *easy* on yourself. We can be lenient, very lenient. You have only to answer this one simple question: "What is the location of the newest tunnel?"' He leaned over Hesburgh, proffering the package of cigarettes; and winking broadly and conspiratorially at Spoor, who stood back of the Senator, Zook purred, 'Cigarette?'

Hesburgh began it again. 'I am the—'

'Silence, stubborn dog!' bawled Zook. Then at Spoor: 'Sergeant Mueller!'

Spoor clicked his heels and popped to attention. '*Jah, mein Colonel!*'

Zook, with cold-eyed cruelty, pointed down at a tunnel opening. 'Take him down to Level Eight!'

'Level *Eight*?' echoed Spoor with feigned horror.

'Level Eight!'

Spoor took him down into the tunnels.

Shortly afterward, Syntax arrived. At the door, Krebs eyed him with horror, for he was still in inmates' garb. 'What the hell is this, Halloween?' snapped the General. 'Where in the hell is the Senator?'

Krebs had no answers. Nor did Cutshaw, as at that moment he re-entered the mansion, and became apprised of the situation. 'Where in the devil is Colonel Kane?' croaked Syntax.

Krebs went after Kane while Cutshaw raced to the inmates' dorm.

Lastrade arrived, bellowing. Then saw the dogs; the holes in the floor; Corfu's mad ceiling; the Nazi uniforms. His thunder shook the mansion, and when he learned that Hesburgh was missing, he said not a word; which frightened Syntax more than anything.

Krebs pounded at Kane's door. It was locked. No answer. Then he and another inmate prowled the mansion, seeking the missing commander.

Spoor had reappeared and now sat grimly in the chair formerly occupied by the Senator. His arms were folded defiantly as Cutshaw tipped the interrogation light full into his face, demanding, 'What have you done with the Senator?'

Spoor said, 'I *told* you! I repossessed him!'

'Where *is* he?'

'The Home Office!'

Cutshaw cuffed his neck, as General Syntax, brooding in the background, muttered, 'Waves! Listen to the waves!'

Cutshaw had despatched the rest of the inmates into the tunnels and around the mansion; sent them feverishly seeking the Senator. Bemish was checking rooms, and went directly to Fell's to explain what had happened. Fell surfaced briefly from his alcoholic daze, said 'Um-hm,' and left his room. He turned a corner of the second-floor landing, walked to a dead-end in the alcove, pressed a stud and looked around furtively as the secret panel slid back. He quietly slipped into the passageway.

In the room off the secret passageway that Spoor had earlier discovered, Senator Hesburgh and Consuelo Endicott sat on a bench in front of the confined dummy of Slovik. She was saying, 'We loved each other madly. Hm. But the studio wouldn't, uh, allow it – no, wouldn't let us marry. "Millions of women love Bela!" they said, "and his public wants him single!"'

Hesburgh's eyes were darting nervously. Spoor had dumped him into this chamber, and then this madwoman had entered with roses. And a story. Good *Lord*, what a story!

'Bela was gone most of the time,' she prattled on, 'and I – uh – was sick with boredom. You see? Yes, sick. Sick with – boredom. What did I say?'

'You were sick with boredom.'

'Oh, yes. So he built this little school for me. Something to, uh, keep me busy. Meantime these passages held us together and away from prying eyes. Eyes *do* pry. Don't you think?'

'Can you open that door?'

But Miss Endicott was oblivious. 'Ah, Bela, darling Bela! In this shrine I keep his memory alive. You understand?'

Abruptly the effigy sat up in its coffin, croaking 'I love you!' and then sat back.

'He *is* alive!' yipped Hesburgh.

Again the Slovik dummy sat up. And again it said, 'I love you!'

Miss Endicott smiled, and put a reassuring hand over the Senator's as the effigy repeated its performance. 'No, no, no; it's just a clock. That and a tape of Bela's voice. Such a comfort in my loneliness. Or, I should say, *former* loneliness.'

'Does anyone else know about this room?'

'Yes, Norman, darling Norman. That's Doctor Norman Fell.' Miss Endicott's eyes turned dreamy. 'It was here that I first met him – amid the stakes and silver bullets. Oh, how terribly ironic. Poor, poor Bela, always worried about his "image". Always hated him for that. Now here I am protecting *mine*.'

The secret panel suddenly slid back. Hesburgh looked up at the figure now framed in the doorway. 'Doctor Fell, I presume?' he said.

'Have you well in a matter of days,' said Fromme.

Cutshaw was still searching. But some of the inmates had given up, squatting despondently on the main hall floor as General Lastrade roundly laced Syntax. 'While we're waiting for the FBI,' rumbled Lastrade, 'would you care to make a statement?'

No one noticed the distant crashing of shoulder against door.

'It was an honest mistake!' yipped Syntax.

'Splendid progress!' bored Lastrade. 'This mansion in ruins, the Gestapo running wild and a United States senator kidnaped! Anything *else*, you splendid ass?!'

'Well,' said Syntax fatuously, 'I believe you left out Kane.'

'I'm *coming* to Colonel Kane! And so's a court-martial! I'm going to—!'

Lastrade abruptly fell silent, staring in shock at the second-floor balcony. Manfred Cutshaw was slowly walking out of Colonel Kane's room, stopping at the balustrade. Tears coursed down his cheeks. He was carrying Kane in his arms. 'He's killed himself,' he said.

Kane's collar was turned around.

"... This Place"

CHAPTER FOURTEEN

Winter melted to spring. Fragrance of flowers, of green things renewing, drifted with wonder and questioning tendrils through the empty Slovik mansion, quickly disbanded in the wake of inquiries following Colonel Kane's suicide. An Air Force staff car pulled up and Captain Cutshaw emerged. It was April and he wore his blues. Within a month after the tragedy, he and all of the mansion's inmates had been fully restored to duty. Cutshaw had asked for a special week's leave.

He looked up at the mansion, the gaping gargoyles, then slowly turned and stared out at the courtyard. Voices wafted to him on the wind . . . 'Simon says . . . Simon says.' He turned and walked into the mansion.

It had not been restored. Holes gaped in the floor. The ceiling was just as Corfu had left it. Cutshaw's eyes felt at the hall, every corner, every chair. Then he slowly walked upstairs. For a moment he paused outside Kane's old room. A sudden impulse urged him to knock. And he did, very softly. Then he gently opened the door and walked inside. He stared down at the bed. It had been stripped, but blood stained the mattress. Slashed wrists; that meant he'd died slowly with time to think; perhaps regret; perhaps forgive. Cutshaw's fingers rubbed at his eyes. He moved to the window, looked out at the sky. A setting sun bathed the wood with glory, caressing the branches of trees with gold. What a beautiful time of day, he thought; sunset; always so beautiful.

He'd visited Fell three days before. The medic was stationed at Bolling Field now, in Washington, D.C. They'd greeted one another cheerily. Then came the pauses in conversation; the embarrassed looks at the floor. Then Cutshaw had asked bluntly if Kane had ever told him anything that might clarify what had happened.

'I know what you're after,' Fell had answered. 'You want to know who killed him; you're afraid it was you. Sure, let's face it. I thought it myself. I mean, about me. I thought it was me. God, any *quack* should have recognized the symptoms.' He paused for a while, then said quietly: 'He was looking for me that night.'

'It wasn't your fault,' Cutshaw had assured him.

'I don't know,' Fell had answered. 'I don't know; I don't know. But he'd be the last one to think it was *any* of us. He blamed something else.' Then he lifted his eyes to Cutshaw. 'He told me something once.'

'What?'

'He said that — "we weren't meant for this place." And that's the reason people went crazy.'

Cutshaw stared out at the sunset, putting the jigsaw puzzle together. Then his glance turned to the bed. He'd found a book beside the body; a text on psychiatric methods. It had been opened – and heavily underlined – at a section devoted to 'shock treatment'.

Cutshaw left the mansion. He drove to the church where he'd gone to Mass that day and asked to see the pastor. He had never trusted priests; they were salesmen, had something to sell. But there was something he had to know.

There had just been a benediction and he met the

old priest in the sacristy. He was taking off his vestments. He recognized Cutshaw's name. 'Spoke of you often,' he said; 'often. Lord, poor man; poor, poor man.'

'What did he say?'

The priest was undoing his cincture. 'Said you had problems. Theology. Don't we all, God knows, don't we all.'

'Did you give him the answers?'

'Lord, not me. I'm a servant of God, my friend, but a poor one. Answers! Lord! There's so much mystery.' He folded away his alb.

Cutshaw produced the letter that Kane had written the night of his death. He handed it to the priest. 'How about this? This come from you?'

The priest read it slowly, cracked lips forming words. Then he looked up. 'That had never occurred to me. But it's good – I think it's good.' He handed back the note. And smiled very thinly. 'Very like him, that. Had a gift for unlikely relationships. He told you his theory of madness?'

'No.'

'Blamed it on Original Sin. Said there's a part of us that remembers what we were like before the Fall – good, in a good world. Then something happened, he said – changed. Trying to cope with the new conditions – evil, pain and disease – earthquakes and matter gone mad – that's what does it – drives us all mad – some more, some less. Fish out of water, he said – alive but – well – out of our minds with the pain of adjustment.' The priest eyed his shoes and tugged at his nose. 'He said that evil doesn't spring out of madness – that it's the other way around.' The pastor looked up at

Cutshaw, some faint memory tugging delicately at his eyes. 'He said we were Ingrid Bergman in *Gaslight* and the Devil is Charles Boyer. Have you any idea what he meant?'

Cutshaw didn't know.

They chatted in amiabilities. Then as Cutshaw was leaving, he turned again at the door. 'Do you think he's – damned?'

'What, son?'

'Damned. He took his own life, but – well, he was mad. At the end, you know, he was mad.'

'God only knows. God only knows. Leave it to Him and to His mercy.'

The old priest paused as he took off his collar, staring off into empty space. 'He was a killer. Or so he said. Son, is it true? He killed eighty-two men?'

'Yes.'

'Yes. That's what he said; whenever he saw me, that's what he said: "Father, I've killed. I'm a killer of men."'

Cutshaw fingered the edge of the doorjamb, fixing his eyes on a statue of Christ. 'He was a lamb.'

Two months later, shod in space suit, Cutshaw waited in his capsule. Headset crackling, he started countdown.

'All systems go!' he said.

And hurtled to the stars.